D1253603

DATE DUE

PRINTED IN U.S.A.

Fort's Law

Fort's Law

JOE L. HENSLEY

PUBLISHED FOR THE CRIME CLUB BY
Doubleday
NEW YORK
1987

All of the characters in this book
are fictitious, and any resemblance
to actual persons, living or dead,
is purely coincidental.

Library of Congress Cataloging-in-Publication Data

Hensley, Joe L., 1926–
Fort's law.

I. Title.
PS3558.E55F6 1987   813'.54   87–13484
ISBN 0-385-23830-4

Fort's Law

I had a three o'clock hearing on a default dissolution in front of a traveling special judge. The case had started out being a "hard" divorce, but after my client had "won" a hearing on a temporary order for custody, things had gotten easier. Her husband had fired his lawyer. I'd waited out the time, gotten it set, and notified the respondent husband, plus my client. When the husband had not shown up, all matters had moved swiftly.

I saw Abe enter through the courtroom doors as we were finishing. He had two women with him. One of them seemed very old, one was possibly fortyish. I'd not seen them before in the office, so they had to be new clients. Abe nodded solemnly at me and I winked back. The two women sat down on the courtroom benches for a while and watched.

Abe nodded also at the special judge who smiled back at him. It was a seldom visitor who didn't know Abe. I got my judgment signed by an affable judge who'd discovered the trial he'd thought might take an hour had only taken short minutes. I gave my client her signed copy and made her happy, or as happy as clients get in these days of sue everyone including your lawyer. This litigant urge has been fed and honed by second-guessers and greedy lawyers, out for a fast insurance buck and a full trial schedule.

I wondered briefly about who the women Abe had in tow were, but there were titles for me to check for the building and loan and so I went though the work for that until it neared four: auditor's office, then the recorder, then county clerk, checking, checking.

I walked back from the crumbling courthouse using an old umbrella that had seen better days. It managed to protect minor parts of me from the cold fall rain.

Scannelsville, Indiana, on a late November Monday, smelled of dead leaves, mud, and the Ohio River at flood stage. I smelled of underarm deodorant (fading), a damp wool suit, and faintly of Canadian whiskey, taken for medicinal purposes (and bad dreams) the night before. I consciously tried not to limp and hoped I was successful. I'd seen palmier days. A few near-the-courthouse merchants watched me suspiciously in apparent agreement.

There were two bars in the block between courthouse and office. I declined to cross the street to either of them for instant healing. I hastened on toward the rundown old building I shared with other renters and Abe, the aging lawyer who owned it. The building held a laundromat, a secondhand bookstore, two upstairs apartments, and our first-floor, shotgun-style (with hall) law offices.

It was now almost four o'clock and I was tired and both my legs hurt.

It had been raining for three straight days. No place looks its best after a three-day rain and Scannelsville, Indiana, was no exception. The streets, seldom overcrowded even at Christmas time, were almost deserted.

At the corner I could look down through the mist and see the Ohio River. It was high, lapping against its bank within a foot of Front Street. The water looked cold and was full of drift. The river had flooded the lowlands and backed up into the creeks that fed it, closing a few of the independent mines in the flood plain.

Many of the area coal mines on both sides of the river had already been closed before the high waters due to other problems, high sulphur mostly, plus some wildcat strikes. The city docks were devoid of barges. In spite of that, the bars I'd passed had appeared to enjoy good crowds of dour men. When the mines were down, it was like that. Sit on a bar stool and slowly drink a beer, husbanding it. Raise hell about national, state, and local government, the mine owners, the democrats and republicans. Then go home and start a fight with the wife. Make a full day of the routine.

A woman sat waiting on one of the hard chairs in our waiting room. Seeing her was a surprise, although I'd known she was around. I'd seen her before, the first time a dozen years back when she'd worn a Navy nurse's uniform. She still looked to me about the same as she'd looked then, lovely. She was one of the reasons I'd come to Scannelsville, although I liked to believe the principal reason was that I'd tired of the big, noisy city of Chicago three hundred plus miles to the north where I'd once practiced. I wondered if she'd remember me if I tried to recall for her the first time I'd seen her. What's important and stands out to one person is most times forgotten by others.

The secretary had abandoned her typewriter. Frannie came in semi-promptly at eight and was gone by three.

Back in his office I could hear Abraham Sapenstein moving around, probably surprised by the woman in the waiting room and wanting to know about why she was there. At seventy-eight years old his curiosity remained strong.

I was "associated" with him. I paid him rent each

month and also paid a minor part of the expenses of the office. For that I got a room of my own, use of the telephone, all the law books I could read, and my name below his on the sign outside the office door. It read "Sapenstein and Fort, Attorneys."

In addition to the money I paid him, he got someone who could fill in when he took his annual January to March bridge and sun vacation in Florida. He was a fanatic bridge player, king of the Scannelsville-area duplicate jousts. He abominated cold weather, so he abdicated his throne in winter and went south to Clearwater. Our association was a good deal for him, a better one for me.

"Are you Mr. Fort?" the woman asked, rising. She was tall, almost as tall as me. Her eyes shone in the light from the front window. They were royal blue, like summer sun on deep water. I remembered those eyes from the hospital ship and the first time I'd seen them. She was beautifully structured and seeing her made my blood pulse more quickly. She was dressed in something half-a-shade darker than her eyes and it fit her cunningly. Her hair was black and curly and very alive. Her features were vivid with perfectly carved lips, a long nose that just failed being patrician, and a chin with the tiniest of clefts.

"I'm Fort," I admitted. I'd thought one day we might meet again and I'd planned my response for that imagined and hoped-for time. Now I could remember nothing of the plans.

"Could you talk with me? I've someone over in jail who needs a lawyer. Your name was given me by Judge Westley."

"All right. Come back to my office, Mrs. DeAlter."

Her eyes widened. "Do we know each other?"

"I know a little about you and Jesse DeAlter. I've seen

you around." I had seen her at a distance, but never her husband. He moved in a different crowd than I did. "It's a small town."

She followed me to my office. I sat her in a chair on the far side of my desk and went to my own chair and waited. She examined me curiously, perhaps still surprised I'd known her.

"If you know who I am, then maybe you know about the trouble Jesse's in?"

"I've heard it's alleged he has drug and drinking problems and I read a few days back in the local paper that he may have sold some drugs to an undercover state police officer. Cocaine. I don't know the exact charge or charges he's in jail on. There are several charges that can be filed when someone possesses or sells cocaine. Some of them are serious."

"This one is serious," she said. "Judge Westley set his bond at a hundred thousand cash or surety dollars this morning. He said Jesse could get twenty years." She looked away, shaking her head, and then back. "Then he also said in court that there's a grand jury meeting about Jesse's aunt's death."

"I see," I said, not seeing. I'd heard the grand jury was in session, but I didn't know (or much care) why. Grand juries are the creatures of prosecutors and do, by the nature of the beast, pretty much what prosecutors tell them to do. I had little use for the local prosecutor or his grand jury. In the several confrontations I'd had with Albert Lawrence (Al) Windham, the circuit prosecutor, I'd found him to be overbearing, loud, bellicose, and often either unprepared or incompetent. He carried a grudge well and had one against me.

"What about Jesse's aunt?" I asked.

"She died last week. I guess they're looking into the way she died. She and Jesse argued a lot. She was an arrogant old coal bitch. She hated me and I despised her."

"How long have you been married, Mrs. DeAlter?" I asked.

"We were married eight years. We got divorced earlier this year, last spring, but he moved in and out some afterward and he kept after me to remarry him." She looked away again, perhaps not used to sharing her private life with a strange man. "Someone has to look out for Jesse just now. I guess I'm all there is."

"Hasn't he got any family?"

"No one close. No one who gives a damn."

"How about friends?"

"A few who were like he was. Druggies, drinkers, bums." She thought for a moment. "There were a couple of brothers he was around a lot. Del Clarkson and another Clarkson, I forget the second one's name. Jesse hung out with them, mostly at Will's Coop, down on Ferry Street above the river. But they'd not have any money or use it to help Jesse if they did."

"You understand you're not legally obligated to help him either?" I asked.

She shrugged.

"Why'd you divorce him if you're still involved with him?"

"It seemed the thing to do. Jesse could live free and comfortable with his aunt and I didn't have the day to day worry of coming home from work to an apartment with Jesse and the Clarksons and others, assorted sexes, laying around inside, drinking or doping. It never was that much of a marriage."

"But still you want to help him?"

She nodded.

"What can you tell me about Jesse's aunt?"

"Her name was Ruth DeAlter. She had a stroke in the summer. She stayed in the hospital for a spell, but she had to get back home. I know she pestered and picked at the doctors until they released her. Then Jesse moved out on me to live with her again." She smiled as if the moving in and out was a joke we now shared. "Ruth lived in that huge family mausoleum on Main Street, the one that looks as if it was built by Queen Victoria after a monthlong drunk. The family castle. Coal money built it. The lives of men like my father built it. There's a closed shaft in the backyard where the DeAlters opened their first mine. Ruth possessed that house and it possessed her. Eighteen rooms. Two live-in servants plus Jesse for genteel things like fetching tea and playing gin rummy. She died a week ago. Someone anonymous called me afterward and said she'd been smothered and did I know Jesse did it. Someone else called and told me everyone in town knew Jesse overdosed her on pills and booze. I guess maybe those same someones also called the prosecutor and got him agitated. Or maybe he's just making noise because he wrote her will, has the estate, and needs to get her death all neat and tidy."

"Male or female callers?"

"I don't know for sure. But two different people. Both with voices maybe muffled by something held over their phone mouthpieces."

"Was Jesse living in her house the night she died?"

"Yes. And I guess he admitted to the police he was in and out of her room. He'd started getting spaced out again and she was home from the hospital. He was talking about trying it again with me, but I couldn't see any hope for it.

We had a fight, him looking down on me socially, me looking down on his drinking, drugs, and friends. So he moved out of my place and back in with her. She'd let him do that. That way she could have a pretty man to cheat at gin rummy, drink with, and use for errands." She nodded to herself, intent on the story. "Not that she needed him much what with two people there in the house who'd worked for her for years."

"An errand boy who was on drugs?" I asked, raising my eyebrows.

"Yes. Better than no one. Better than servants. It's an old family. Jesse's very pretty. Ruth had tons of money, but hated spending it. Old coal money. Money maybe from Michael DeAlter, Jesse's father, stolen when Michael lost his memory and then died. Jesse can look good when he tries and he's real bright." She smiled, perhaps remembering good times. "Jesse wrote a novel once, Mr. Fort. A lot of critics took it seriously and said it was a good book and that he had promise. They said he was someone to watch, a comer. Then he got himself into drugs and his world slowed down. Now he sits at a typewriter when he's sober and straight and stares for hours, not typing a thing. Or maybe he'll do a sentence or a paragraph and then get mad and throw it in the wastebasket."

"When you were living with him, what did you do to feed the both of you?" I asked, knowing.

She examined me. "I'm not sure why you want to learn all these things, but I'm an R.N. I work at the Scannelsville Hospital and it pays okay."

"All right. And you want to hire me to look into Jesse's situation?"

"Not exactly. I told Judge Westley I didn't have any money or property except a few pieces of beat-up furniture plus my salary and that Jesse, at least for now, didn't either. He talked real easy to me and said I was to pay you what I could and the county would pay the rest." She searched through her purse and found a worn billfold. "I could give you a hundred dollars now," she said. "Then you're supposed to keep track of your hours. Judge Westley said you'd been counsel like that before and would know what to do." She looked away and then back. "I paid one lawyer to get rid of Jesse and then didn't have enough sense to leave it like that, so I guess I'm stuck."

"How about Jesse? You mentioned a Michael who was his father. Is there money for him sometime? Like maybe a trust?"

"No. Either Michael died poor or Ruth stole his money before or after he died. Jesse will get it back now from her estate maybe. He should, but then you never know."

"All right," I said. "I'll take a look at what Jesse's into and then get in touch with you tomorrow. Put your name, address, and telephone number on a card for me." I dug in a drawer, found a client card, and handed it to her.

She gave me five twenties. I wrote her a receipt for the money and gave it to her. She accepted gravely. Our hands touched briefly and my hand burned from the contact. *My old flame, who'd probably never known I existed!*

She filled out the card. I sat watching and she seemed uncomfortable with me watching, but I watched anyway. It had been a long time since I'd been able to look at her. She'd not changed a lot. A bit older, a few lines under her eyes, and maybe five pounds lighter for perfection. It was nice to look.

When she was done she handed me the card. I took it and put it in the thin client file I maintain.

"You make me nervous," she said. "Do I know you from

somewhere?" She got up from her chair, curious about me, perhaps sensing some of my intensity. "I get this feeling that maybe we met someplace. Did we?"

I smiled at her and ignored the question. "I'll call you tomorrow."

I watched her walk out of the office and into the rain. She opened one of those plastic umbrellas you can see through. She turned back once at the curb and looked back at me watching her from the window. Then she shook her head and crossed the street. Her car was a ten-year-old Ford, rusting in the rain.

When the car was gone from sight, I walked back to Abe's office. He sat behind his desk, an aging man without a lot to interest him except the world that he knew, Scannelsville. His wife had died five years back. He had no children, no close relatives. Now and then he'd drive into Evansville on Saturdays with Doc Jacobsen for synagogue, but even that was sporadic and seemed to mean little to him.

His eyes were faded but inquisitive. "You're going to get yourself into a murder trial if you mess with that pretty, Jack." He nodded and hummed a little tune to himself. "I took some ladies who are interested in the town's old families over to show them the records in the basement and heard around that prosecutor Al is out after Jesse DeAlter like a hunting dog after a three A.M. coon."

"Just now all they've charged him with is a drug sale to a state cop. Judge Westley appointed me on that."

"By tomorrow it'll be murder, you mark what I say. Lots of folks in the courthouse were talking about it. Surely someone over there said something to you about it."

I shrugged. "I didn't ask. I did my title work and a

divorce. And in addition I don't care what they gossip about in the courthouse. Someone's got to defend him, whether or not."

"Al Windham already don't like you. You get your fanny out in his big pig way in this one and he'll stomp you clear through the floor. He's a ruthless man. The word I hear is he's going after Judge Westley's job in next year's election. Al don't like to lose. He'll go to great lengths to avoid it. The local bar don't like him, but he's cunning and they're right careful with him. You should be that way also if you want to be locally successful." He watched me, grinning his false-toothed grin, trying to egg me into an argument. I knew him well enough to know that he lived for legal times like this. He wrote wills and checked mortgages and did tax work for his excellent living, but when he told stories, it was always about big criminal cases he'd touched at their fringes. Helped pick the jury, did research, took witness statements, was deputy prosecutor.

I thought I knew what it was he wanted. "You going to help me out in this?"

He nodded. "Sure. Sure I will, even if it cuts some into my sun time." He looked down at his watch. "My, ain't it late. Let's go get us a drink or three somewhere."

"If I buy the drinks, will you tell me something about the DeAlters and those connected with them?"

"You bet I will," he said, delighted. "If I heard right, you got a piece of money up front?"

I smiled at him and nodded. I liked him about as well as I'd ever like anyone. He'd made a small fortune by being a meticulous detail man, a man who wrote unbreakable contracts, never made a mortgage mistake, and kept his legal word. I knew Scannelsville, a county-seat town of nine thousand, and its fifteen lawyers liked him. When I'd first come into his office, he'd seemed old and sick, slow of speech, unsteady of gait, and bad of color. Now he seemed healthy again and looked good for a few more years. He could drink half a bottle of sour mash and never lose control of his tongue. And he knew most of the town's secrets. I thought maybe a part of his recovery might be because he'd enjoyed seeing me cut a small swath in the area's courtrooms. I wasn't bad in court. Maybe not that good either, but I filled a need in him.

We closed and locked the office and walked down the street to Pajama's Place. It was the elite place to drink if you weren't country club. Drinks at Pajama's were a quarter more than in the coal miners' bars. Behind the bar and on the walls of Pajama's Place they had glued pictures of women in various types of sleeping gear. Nothing wild. No men's magazine stuff, but just the kind of pictures you could cut out of the myriads of women's magazines. Provocative, but pure. No nudes and no bathing suits. You could take a date to Pajama's. Several times I'd taken local girls in and they'd at least professed to like the place, although most of them had resisted returning to be faced with all those sleepy beauties.

A few other townsmen were already present when we entered. Several hailed Abe and nodded at me. Abe smiled and played the clown for them. Usually we sat with them at the long bar and listened to the lies of the day, but tonight Abe waved his way past and led me to a booth in the far rear of the bar. I nodded an order at bent, ten-gallon-hatted Killer Kilgore. He was the bartender-owner and was said to be in his nineties. Some said he wore the hat to hide a bald head. I'd never seen him with it off. In a few moments he brought Abe a Jack and tall water and me a goodly splash of Canadian Club on the rocks.

"You know the family?" I asked Abe when Killer was gone. "The DeAlters?"

"All my life. In Ruth's generation there were only two left. Ruth and her dead brother, Michael. Ruth never married. The town says she never found anyone good enough. Michael married twice, maybe to make up for it. His first wife died of cancer and he married again. She also died, in a car accident. Tragic. There was one child out of each marriage, Jesse being out of the second. Michael ran the mines. He was a Purdue graduate. After he died, Ruth tried to run things. When that didn't work, she leased out the mines to big companies and stopped caring about them."

"And Jesse?"

"She had all the money and I'll bet Jesse wanted it." He shook his head philosophically. "I'd guess first off, and this town will also guess, that Jesse done the dirty deed, Jack."

"Did Jesse ever work at a job?"

"Sort of. When he came back from Canada after hiding out up around Toronto during Vietnam, he tried some college over east for a while. Then he wrote that book of his and some of the high-class people in town were scandalized. It was about a big-money coal mining family, a rebellious second son, a cruel father, and a nutty aunt and half brother, very thinly disguised. Mean book. I read it and liked it." He smiled. "There's a sneaky lawyer in it that's got to be partly me. Then, when there weren't any more books in Jesse after number one, he started up a bookstore. You could drink coffee and tea and talk to kindred spirits there. It died. Not enough readers in Scannelsville except for the Playboy crowd. So, nothing. Drinking and drugs. I seen Jesse a few times with the Clarkson brothers. Bad news."

"Why bad news?"

"They've been in trouble all their lives. Stealing, house-breaking, burglaries, that sort of thing."

"Maybe they'd be good candidates for whoever did Ruth in?"

"Sell it to the prosecutor, not to me," Abe said.

"I might try. Back to Jesse. He was into drugs. Selling or using?"

"Both, or that's what you'd hear. Been going on for years. He married that girl, Karen. She's a nurse. Pretty and smart, but no family worth a local damn. Her daddy was a shift foreman or something out at the Big Otto and died in an underground cave-in years ago. The mother was a local yokel, pretty, but country. Karen came out with brains, God knows from where. She lifted herself by her own bootstraps. Ruth DeAlter was scandalized when they got married. She booted Jesse out. Then she took him back later. My reports about it are that the conditions of the taking back were that he couldn't have Ruth and the big house and afternoon teas plus Karen. When he was on the outs with Karen, then Ruth would let him move back in, but when he was living with Karen, then Miss Ruth wanted nothing to do with him." He lifted his glass and inventoried the contents. "And so it continued with him getting more and more into booze and drugs and proba-bly less and less into Karen until she finally divorced him." He grinned, a dirty old man and proud of it.

"What was Ruth like?"

"Meaner than a miscarrying mole. Smart and vicious. A manipulator. When she was young, she was a lot for looks, a handsome lady. I don't think time ever changed that self-vision inside her rock head. She thought she was still the belle of the ball as she got older. Very narcissistic. Very autocratic. Went to Louisville, Evansville, and Indianapolis to buy her clothes and to see plays and operas and symphonies. Cultured. But she could cuss worse than a late-shift coal miner." He nodded, remembering. "I was at her house for a dinner party maybe three or four years back. I used to do a very small piece of her work. Not recent. Al Windham's her latest lawyer. She ran through a lot of us. Jesse was cohosting the party and acting as high as Ruth did. And Karen wasn't there, of course. Jesse and Ruth were very close that year. Unhealthy."

"Are you telling me that Jesse was sleeping with his now deceased old auntie?"

"I don't know and refuse to do any guessing about what was going on. I'll only say that I think he was doing something she wanted, something evil, trading whatever she asked for safe haven and the promise of future money. His father Michael, in some way no one at the time understood, died broke."

"I heard that, but tell me more."

"Michael was a very secretive man, senile and sick in his last years. The town theorized that maybe there were bad business deals no one here knew of. There were large withdrawals from the bank, stocks and bonds sold, and cash obtained. When he died, there was nothing to be found. He'd put his mine stock in Ruth's name. She said it was for a loan. And the house was in joint title with rights of survivorship to Ruth, so she got that. They searched, they took pictures of Michael to area banks looking for lockboxes, and they checked the house, but nothing turned up."

"And never has?"

"Right."

I found that interesting, but it was ancient history now. "Tell me what you know about Ruth's death?"

"You hear different stories. Most say she was suffocated and maybe drugged up front. She had a bad heart and she'd had a stroke. She took pills and potions by the basket. There's some speculation that a someone substituted the wrong medicine and stopped her heart, but most are holding out for the smothered theory. You could talk to my friend Doc B. J. Jacobsen, the county coroner."

"He's your friend," I said. I didn't have much use for Jacobsen or he for me. He'd been Abe's closest friend before I came to town. Perhaps it was that. "You said you'd help, so you talk to him."

He nodded, old eyes sparkling. "Okay. I'll do that. Me and Doc go back a long ways. He's been touting me on bad horses for fifty years."

"Guess for me, Abe. Why would Al the prosecutor be so damned sure Jesse killed her?"

"My bet is he ain't. But Jesse was staying in the house and I've heard his room adjoined hers. You can bet there'll be evidence of fights and threats and further evidence that Jesse was stoned or boozed to the eyeballs on the fatal night. Plus people figure Jesse wanted her money." He looked away and then back. "It's the kind of case Al likes, one where he can shout and point the finger. He'll find enough and then have himself a circus."

"Could be. What else do you know?"

"Let me think on it. Overnight I might remember more, especially should you oil my memory glands a bit." He frowned out at Killer Kilgore and then complained: "Does that old bastard think we're camels?"

I dreamed that night. I dreamed of flames and falling from the sky, the parachute burning toward the last of the fall, of the helicopter coming for me and pulling me from the sea. My dream soon became a nightmare and my legs were gone, burned away. I was about to die.

The damaged parachute had slowed me enough. In my nightmare it didn't.

I saw Karen DeAlter's face through a mist. I was aboard the hospital ship and she was there close, but it made no difference. I was going to die. Death was a new beginning, feared, but certain.

Then, at the end, she took my hand and whispered to me and it was a dream again and I was alive. My legs grew back, gone one second, regrown the next.

I lived.

Twice I awoke with muscle spasms, but in the way of such things, when the spasms relaxed, I'd find my way back to the dream, some things changed, some the same. But Karen was always far away in the new dreams. I'd catch a glimpse of her and she'd be gone, vanished in the mist.

I was glad when morning came.

In the morning, after some calisthenics including sit-ups and push-ups, I walked my daily three miles. The doctors had advised me about walking when they let me leave the last hospital, although the distance then recommended had been much less. At first, in the hospitals, it had been a few feet, later all the way down a hall, then a block. My regimen now was three miles and sometimes farther.

I remembered those first days when I'd held onto the steel exercise bar above my hospital bed with clenched

hands and willed the pain to go away, the days I lifted and
sank on the bar, wondering if the legs would ever work
again.

The doctors had wanted me to stay on for more therapy
and perhaps other operations, had said such treatment
would be beneficial to me. I'd talked my way out when I
could walk well enough to get around. I'd promised them
I'd stay around as an outpatient, but once out, I'd taken
the first plane to Chicago. I had no intention of ever returning to the hospital. If they tried to put me back, then
they could fight me for the disability pension. If they won,
that would be all right. No one was going to cut on me
again. Not for legs anyway.

I had money, more than enough to keep me if I never
worked. When my mother and father had died in the
commercial airline crash, there'd been money. I'd rather
have had them alive, but it wasn't to be, so now I had
money.

They'd lived their comfortable lives in a suburb near
Chicago. Then they were gone. They'd died when I was in
the second of the three Navy hospitals, and I'd not been
allowed or able to go to their funerals. A long time after
their deaths I'd visited their graves, where they lay side
by side, and seen their stones. I knew, from news stories,
that their plane had hit a mountain and burned, so the
stones were what was left.

I got away from that. It's easy to be sorry about what's
happened to you, to cry about how you've been wounded,
and what you've lost. It's hard to keep on, to search, and to
work, but it's an answer.

The weather outside had changed. The sky still looked
threatening, but it had stopped raining. It had grown
noticeably colder, maybe in the high thirties. Now and

then a single flake of snow would float past. The *Farmer's Almanac* had predicted an early and hard winter. I'd heard that from both the courthouse and the co-op crowd, from people who kept me up on things like tobacco prices, the intricacies of coal mining, and sometimes whispered various tidbits of local gossip.

I'd dressed warmly, but I'd forgotten my gloves. I shoved my hands into the deep pockets of my coat and tried to keep them warm that way.

I walked from my apartment near the west end of Main Street on up towards downtown. A few blocks away from the business section I cut south and walked along the river, staying on the water side of the street and away from the tobacco warehouses. The water was now falling, down a foot from yesterday. When I'd checked out the river, I walked back up toward the courthouse. Scannelsville merchants broomed sidewalks outside their stores and talked animatedly with each other. Better weather could mean business. Even with the coal mines mostly shut down or working skeleton crews there'd soon be tobacco sales and that would bring in spending money. I nodded at some of the merchants and some who knew me or knew of me nodded back, appraising my clothes. Maybe they could tell by quick inspection I'd bought the clothes in Chicago while I was working there. *Expensive city clothes!*

The walking was easy enough now. I could do it without a lot of pain and when I wanted, I could force myself to do it without a limp. The right leg was the worst one, but now I couldn't tell a lot of difference. It cramped more than the left, but that seemed the only added symptom.

The jet fighter had been burning when we'd parted company high over Cape Dinh. Some of the fuel and flames had gotten on my legs and my parachute. It had been mostly third-degree burns from the lower thighs down. I'd spent the early time in the hospital ship sedated, bandaged like a mummy, even my face covered. But now I could walk and, after a fashion and crab-like, I could run. Fast enough for a small-town lawyer who cared nothing about ambulances.

I passed kids on their way to school. Some of them looked me over curiously, but in the almost-a-year I'd spent in Scannelsville most of them had seen me before and so grown used to me. *The man who walked funny.* In a town of nine thousand plus and a county of thirty thousand, even the kids soon know who everyone is.

I'd not said anything to anyone in the town about Vietnam. No one knew about me, not even Abe. Abe vaguely knew I'd been on a carrier, but that was all. I liked it that way. Nothing's as boring as an old war and smug veterans talking incessantly about it. I'd smilingly endured a lot of battles won, places seen, and drinks liberated in World War II, Korea, and Vietnam in Pajama's without saying anything.

I made the walk work out so I was at the end of three miles when I got to the courthouse.

I was there about the time that Al Windham parked his Cadillac in his marked spot and preceded me through the front door. He refused to notice me and I likewised him. We waited for the elevator without a word.

Al got ponderously off the elevator at two and I rode on to three.

Chicken Abelard, the bailiff, was already in his office. It was his routine to go early to the courthouse and not leave until four, staying later if there was a jury trial.

I grinned at him from outside the door of his cubbyhole.

He was almost as big as the room, vast and spreading, in his late fifties and very strong-looking. He was a deliberate man who seemed to know everyone and was good at his job.

"Morning, Mr. Bailiff," I said. "Look me over. I'm dry. No rain, no umbrella, but it sure feels like winter out there."

"I was outside before I was inside, Fort," he said, smiling. "Coffee?"

We weren't close, but he seemed willing to give me the benefit of his doubts most times. I sensed that the people who were closest to Chicken were people he'd known for a long time. I'd never make it if that was the main requirement. His temper was reputed to sometimes be uncertain, but it had not been so with me. He was a retired cop, twenty plus years on the Scannelsville police. I'd heard that once a large and irate defendant had tried to attack Judge Westley after a divorce case. Chicken had repelled the assault with one blow and broken the man's jaw in two places.

"Coffee would be fine," I said. "I'll get it. Could I get you to dig out the file on Jesse DeAlter meanwhile?"

"Yep. You get your own coffee and I'll run down the file," he said. He frowned. "Grand jury is meeting on him from what I hear. They're to finish deliberations today." He cut his throat with a casual, imaginary knife. "Murder," he said. "Bad stuff."

"I'll cross that bridge when I must. Right now I need to see what he's charged with. Some kind of drug charge?"

"Yep."

I wondered for the hundredth time why they called him "Chicken," but decided again against asking. We got along and there was no sense risking anything to satisfy my curiosity. My father, a careful corporate lawyer, had taught me that.

I went to the library and got a cup of coffee. It was yesterday's without a doubt, black and evil-looking, but hot. I warmed my hands around the cup, bringing them back to life. I had a sip. Strong—like on my carrier in the South China Sea.

Chicken gave me the file. Jesse was charged with selling cocaine. The information had been signed by a state police officer who'd signed his name to the document and then put "ISP" after his name. I read it carefully. The same state police officer was listed as the purchaser. The offense was a "Class B" felony, max sentence twenty years, minimum six, plus a fine of up to ten thousand dollars. I thought it was a crime wherein the sentence could be suspended under certain circumstances. The docket sheet showed there'd been an initial hearing on it yesterday, that Westley had appointed me to represent the defendant, then read him his constitutional rights and set an omnibus date.

I didn't recognize the name of the state police officer who'd signed the information, but they'd not have used one from the Scannelsville post to do their undercover drug work. It would be someone from outside, black, bearded, or both, wearing jeans, waiting to trap the unwary and careless.

I handed the file back to Chicken. "Do you know offhand if Jesse DeAlter has any prior convictions?" Priors could make a difference in whether Jesse was granted a suspended sentence or perhaps shock probation after short prison time.

"I checked. There are a couple of public intoxication things down in county court where he was fined. He drinks." Chicken leaned toward me. "If it weren't for this thing with his aunt, I'd bet that Judge Westley would let him plead out and go to one of those substance-abuse places where they'd try to wean him off drugs—if that's ever possible."

I remembered what Abe had told me. "Abe thinks Al plans to use his case against DeAlter for campaign fodder when he announces against the judge in a few months. Al has to be the logical choice for the opposition party."

Chicken's face darkened. One of the reasons he tolerates me well is that we both have little use for the prosecutor. Chicken thought about what I'd said and then nodded.

"You mean to show how tough and upright he is?" he asked. "How mean and straight and vicious he is?"

"That plus other things. A juicy family murder with big money involved always puts the prosecutor in the limelight. Has anyone from the city newspapers been around looking things over yet?"

"No. But there were some calls yesterday and I'll bet they'll be around."

"Al will get a chance to cavort before the media every day between now and the date Jesse's sentenced—if he's sentenced. You watch and see. We'll not only have a trial, we'll have a two-a-day performance by Al." I smiled. "That's if it works his way."

"Election ain't until next November," Chicken said stolidly. "Not quite a year away."

"Maybe he thinks he can make the show last until then."

Chicken examined me. "I know why I dislike Al, but sometimes I wonder about why you do, Jack. You ain't been here long and you're nothing politically. I know you came here from Chicago. What is it makes you dislike Al? Did you know him someplace before?"

"No. I guess it's just good taste on my part," I said. "I don't like or trust public prosecutors who play out their games for the news media rather than juries. He did it to me in that point-one-oh causing death case I tried against him in the summer. He then had the gall to call a press conference after the jury found my man not guilty. He complained to the media about a verdict that was dead right. If he'd bullied his way through it and won, it would likely have been reversed at the appellate level from what I read in the casebooks. He thereafter got openly irritated with me when I replied in the same news media that if he'd tried his case more competently or filed it for the offense my client committed and would have plead guilty to, he might have served the people better." I smiled. "That burned him. He thought it was going to be easy and he could shout his way through it and then it wasn't."

Chicken grinned, perhaps recalling the case. My defendant had been both drunk and driving, but he'd been drunk on his side of the road and within the speed limit on the nearby interstate. There were several witnesses. A luckless driver going the other way had either gone to sleep or lost control, come across the wide grass median, and hit my drunk driver and so been killed. My defendant had suffered only minor injuries. I'd early offered to plead my man to a simple DUI or .10 misdemeanor and had been haughtily rebuffed. The counteroffer had been for a plea of guilty with an eight-year sentence, four suspended. My client had preferred to take his chances. Al had tried hard. He'd brought in the area organizations against drinking drivers to pack the courtroom after *voir dire.* The jury had rebelled and my man had walked.

Thereafter the judge had ruled that a .10 offense was included in the case and couldn't be filed after the fact. The resultant moments had not been unsweet.

Since then, as in the morning elevator ride, Al and I had enjoyed a nodding acquaintance. He said "nodding" to me and I did vice versa. I'd had other run-ins with him in court, but nothing out of the ordinary. He was the type who thought he could win if he could outshout you. I thought he was both immoral and opportunistic. I figured he was waiting for a chance to rub my nose in it and Jesse DeAlter was that chance. I wondered if he knew I'd been hired/appointed yet. Chances were he did, but Westley had little use for Al, so maybe not.

"Could I see the judge when he gets here?"

Chicken nodded solemnly. "You'll be number one in line." He pulled out a turnip watch and glanced at it. "Soon now."

I thought out loud for him. "I'll file a petition to let to bail, take a look at Al's evidence, and then move for an early trial date. Let's see angry Al make his murder last long then."

Chicken smiled at me. "I'm glad you picked here to settle, Jack. I know the judge is also. Sometimes both of us wonder, along with other locals, why you left a big-city firm where rumor has it you were making lots of bucks and came down here."

"I didn't like what I was doing in Chicago. I've a bit of money and I draw some disability. I don't need much to keep me."

"Your disability, is it your legs?"

"Yes."

"War?"

"I got burned a little once."

He shook his head, not really understanding. Everyone knew you were stupid if you quit a job that paid nearly six figures a year to go to one that paid a small fraction of that, whether you liked job one or not.

I thought he was about to say more, but outside we heard footsteps in the hall.

"Wait," Chicken ordered. He got up and moved around me ponderously. In a few moments he came back.

"He'll see you in chambers."

I walked across the hall and entered Westley's office. He sat smiling at me.

"What's up, Jack?"

"I'd like to have you ask the sheriff to bring Jesse DeAlter over here for me to talk to, Judge."

"Is the jail not good enough?" he asked curiously. He leaned back in his chair. He was a small man, a lot smaller than me. He'd been, I'd heard, a quiet, effective lawyer for a lot of years in Scannelsville. Now he was circuit judge.

I smiled. "Sometimes, over at the jail, I get the feeling that people are listening to every word and maybe reporting back on conversations to the prosecutor, a gentleman who has little use for me."

He sat unmoving, considering what I'd said. I'd found him to be a good judge, willing to listen, willing to be convinced. I liked him. He'd been appointed to fill the unexpired term by the governor when ancient Judge Hiram Johns, whom I'd never known, had dropped dead in open court two years back. Now he was going to have to run to retain office and Al Windham was after him. Next year. I knew who I wanted to win, but I didn't know the town and was uncertain about what would happen. The past political history of the area was that sometimes one party won, sometimes the other.

He opened his desk drawer. "In a moment then we'll call over for him." He rummaged through the drawer and found something. He handed it to me. It was in a plain white envelope. Inside there was a copy of a note.

"I got that regular mail. I think it's possible the prosecutor maybe got the original, what with this being a copy."

The note read: "I seen a big man watching the DeAlter house one night. It wasn't no Jesse."

"When did you get this?"

"A few days ago. The day before the grand jury started its hearings. There'd already been stories about Ruth DeAlter's death in the local papers." He looked out his window and then back. "Over and above the obituary."

"Can I have this? Assuming I'm going to have to defend the murder case?"

"Sure. And you'll be defending the case. Maybe it would be better to let me have Chicken make a copy of this copy instead. At some time in the future you may want to show I did get it. That could be done by calling my court reporter. She routinely opens the mail and the note was in it. It was inside this envelope here and was mailed in a larger envelope, no return address, but a local postmark. She has that envelope also."

"I wonder if the grand jury has seen it?"

He shrugged, not knowing. He pushed a button on his desk and, in a moment, Chicken appeared in the doorway.

"Warm up the copy machine. Make a couple of copies of this for Jack," he directed.

Chicken nodded and took the note.

"Have you seen Jesse DeAlter yet?" Judge Westley asked.

"Not yet. His ex-wife came over late yesterday and told me I'd been appointed in the drug thing and about the possible murder charge. She gave me a hundred dollars up front."

"I set a high bond because murder's not normally bondable. I didn't want Jesse DeAlter out and us having to look for him again. And Windham's been hinting around to the newspeople that he may try for the death penalty."

I raised my eyebrows. "I wonder how he figures to do that?"

Judge Westley smiled.

"The statute, as I remember, spells out about ten aggravating circumstances allowing a prosecutor to file a separate death penalty page," I went on.

The judge nodded gravely. "Perhaps the prosecutor has figured out something we know nothing about. Maybe he could claim Jesse was robbing his aunt?" He avoided my eyes, picked up his phone and got the sheriff's office. "Bring over Jesse DeAlter," he said.

We waited silently. In a few moments Chicken came back. He handed me two copies of the note the judge had shown me. He gave the original back to Judge Westley who put it back into the envelope and then into his desk drawer. I folded my copies and placed them in my inside jacket pocket.

Down at the end of the hall I heard footsteps approaching. A man in handcuffs and manacles clinked past our door. I stepped out into the hall when Judge Westley nodded his permission. One prisoner, two deputies.

Good odds.

I took Jesse DeAlter into the jury room to talk. It was a good place for discussions. The doors and walls were heavy and an overly inquisitive deputy, even if he put his ear against the thick door, would be hard pressed to hear what was being said inside.

DeAlter was an impressive-looking man in his late thirties. Alcohol and drugs hadn't much affected his looks. He was tall and blond with regular features, a heavier Robert Redford look-alike. He wore his chains and the manacles as if they were a sort of costume. His eyes were deep brown, wide, and arrogant. If he suffered any kind of withdrawal symptoms from alcohol or drugs, they weren't apparent to my untutored eyes.

I'd wondered how a woman like Karen could have stayed married and involved with a druggie and/or drunk, but seeing Jesse answered my questions. Physically, he was as perfect in his way as she was in hers.

"My name's John Fort," I said. "People usually call me Jack. Your ex-wife hired me and the court appointed me to be your lawyer."

He looked me over. "Well, I did give a smidge of nose rose to some black guy who wound up being a state cop," he said tolerantly. "That possibly wasn't very smart, was it?"

"No. Very unsmart. Did you give it to the state trooper or sell it to him?"

"I sold it, but for very little more than I'd paid. A friendly deal between supposed friends. And I didn't take the payment then. What difference does it make?"

"At the outer limits twelve years."

"That seems most sanguine," he said, still coolly tolerant.

"How come you took no money at sale time?" I asked.

"I didn't need it then. I like to have some accounts that are due when I need them."

I found the fact that he'd not been paid significant. I said, "The drug charge isn't the worst thing. If it were all there was, we might get you out from under okay, but evidently you're about to be indicted for murder and I'll be defending that also."

He nodded, not surprised. "I heard some things about the murder over in jail. There's a deputy I used to go to school with. Grade-school chums. He didn't much like me then and doesn't now. The feeling, by the way, is mutual. He tells me things he thinks I won't like hearing." He smiled without any meaning. "So they think I did in my Aunt Ruth?" He shook his head slowly. "Why would I do that? It's silly on the face of it. I was living there and she was, after a fashion, paying my way. Why would I want to kill the dear old bat?"

"Maybe for her money," I suggested.

"Oh yes, the money." He looked at me, bored with it all. "How exactly am I supposed to have done her in? The deputy hasn't confided that to me yet. I think he wants me to tell him."

"There are various theories. Overdosed or underdosed her. Changed her medicine. Maybe forced something on her that her old heart couldn't tolerate. The most popular theory is that you, to make sure, smothered her."

Some trace of emotion came in his eyes, but I was unable to read it.

"I didn't do it," he said flatly. "I went into her room like I'd done a thousand times before. I'd been asleep, but I woke up. She was in her bed and I didn't like the look of her, so I got one of the servants. My aunt was dead." He examined me more closely. "So you're what I get for a lawyer. Your clothes look better than most I've seen around here. Rumpled a bit, but good quality. Are you any good at lawyering?"

"Maybe you'd better hope so."

"Maybe's right, and maybe not. It's possible, with Aunt Ruth's money involved, that I could get someone big to come here and take my case. If I win, then they win."

"Do you get her money?"

"Of course. At least I'd certainly presume so." For the first time there was something other than arrogance in his face. I read it as doubt. "I'm her only close heir," he continued. "There are a few distant cousins she despised, but no one else."

"She didn't legally have to leave you a thing. Believe me when I tell you that. And were I you, I'd not tell anyone you ever had any idea she did have to leave you some or all of her money. It's what's called a motive."

"Nevertheless . . ." he began. His voice went lower. "Surely she left her money to me. I've always had a theory she stole my father's money when he got senile and then died, so surely . . ." He stopped.

"Maybe she did leave it to you and you can then hire someone who specializes in criminal law and I can withdraw."

"Can you look into it for me?" he asked, regaining confidence. He lifted his hands together and regarded them. His fingers were long and tapering. He looked handsome and aristocratic even in chains. He was wearing a graying white shirt, but his pants and sport coat were first class. "In the meantime, while we're finding out, I suppose there'll be no problem in you bumbling along." He smiled at me. "Give my dear ex-wife, sweet Karen, my best. Tell her since I've been in jail I've begun to think even more in terms of us together again." He gave me a broad wink.

"I'll do that," I said evenly. "And I'll also bumble about as best I can."

He shook his head, reading me. "I think she's captured you. She does that to almost everyone. I never met a woman with so much animal magnetism." He smiled. "Won't do you any good. She's unimaginative and as cold as a naked witch on a January broom."

"You're my worry, not your ex-wife," I said, not liking him a lot.

"Sure." He grinned a charming grin.

I thought about how I'd dress him for the trial if he'd listen. A dark suit and somber tie. *Elegant! With women, lots of women, on the jury!*

I tapped on the jury-room door. I told Jesse I'd see him again soon and let the deputies take him. I noted that they treated him with a degree of deference. *A born celebrity!*

If he got convicted, I thought he surely could sell his memoirs. After all, it's part of the sensational murder scene these days.

Ruth DeAlter's mansion sat on a full quarter block of land on East Main Street. I'd passed by it going to and from work hundreds of times without wondering much about it.

I keep a car for long-distance travel, but I walk everywhere from my apartment, which is the smaller half of an old home.

Today I looked the DeAlter place over carefully. I walked all the way around its block, seeing parts of the back of the house through other house yards, and seeing the front and side. The mansion was huge and might once have been handsome, but now was only impressive because of its size. It was vine-covered and tree-shaded with lumpy brick walks near the walls and a gazebo, in need of paint, in the side yard. Gargoyles with pitted faces guarded the roof, peering out from beneath eaves. The roof itself seemed to be of heavy slate, cracked here and there. Behind the house there was a small building which once might have been a carriage house and was now a garage. Between it and the house, there was first a fountain and then a raised knoll of brick and stone in the middle of the backyard. Someone had erected a bronze plaque, now gone green, at its apex, but I couldn't read any of it from the sidewalk. The closed mine entrance, I guessed.

Around the mansion, on smaller lots that fronted on Main Street and the side streets, there were smaller, handsomer houses. The DeAlter place stood out because it was so large, an ocean liner in the midst of tugs.

I decided to start with the small houses. Those houses directly across Main Street from the mansion would be the ones which would get the best view of the DeAlter place. I walked to the house which was straight across the street from the DeAlter door. It was a federal-style two-story built almost to the sidewalk, maybe a hundred and fifty years old. Despite the cold of the day a tiny woman in a ragged coat raked resolutely at leaves in her miniature front yard, talking softly to herself and perhaps the leaves as she worked.

There was an iron fence and gate in front of her house. A metal sign attached to the gate read THE HEADLEYS. I stood at the gate waiting until the lady inside noticed me. She stopped raking and leaned on her rake handle.

"Yes?" she asked.

"Are you Mrs. Headley?"

"That's right. I'm pleased you're capable of reading signs, young man. Some in your generation can't."

I disregarded her sharp answer. "My name's John Fort, ma'am. I'm a lawyer. Judge Westley has appointed me to represent Jesse DeAlter."

"I see. Well, you can open up the gate and step inside the yard. My hearing isn't perfect and I don't want to try talking with you out there and me inside here. But you keep your distance while you're inside. I also don't want any of my aristocratic, nosy neighbors to think any impure thoughts." She smiled a little, perhaps intrigued to be a part of the latest town scandal.

I opened her gate and entered. I moved one step inside and stopped.

I thought she was late seventyish. Her face was a mass of prune-like wrinkles, but her eyes were still child bright, able to inspect the world and marvel at its perfidies. "I knew Ruth DeAlter a bit," she said. "Others who live close by and who were more into things with her probably knew her better. I don't go to her church or belong to her sorority and I never neighbored much with her when she was alive. In fact, I didn't like her a lot. She was a heavy drinker for a time. Until she had her stroke, I'd see her staggering around in her yard. I don't hold with using alcohol. But I did know her. I also know and like Karen and know Jesse."

"You'll do just fine. Tell me what you know about Ruth and Jesse," I said.

She shook her head. "That's gossiping and I don't engage in it." She smiled, thinking of a way. "You ask your questions and I'll try to answer them. That way things are strictly business." She sniffed at the cold air, enjoying herself.

I started out easy. "What's the brick and stone mound in the backyard of the house?" I thought I knew from what Karen had said.

"That's the sealed opening to Big Dee Mine Number One. It petered out twenty plus years ago. For a while it was open and kids got in there, so Michael had it sealed and the plaque erected. Coal silliness."

"How long ago did Michael die?"

"Oh dear," she said, thinking. "Years and years. Twenty maybe."

"He was Jesse's father?"

"Yes."

"And how did he die?"

"In a fall. He was to the place where someone had to watch him all the time. He could walk and he was strong, but his mind was gone. He fell in the house someplace, down a flight of steps."

"Tell me about Ruth and Jesse. Did you ever see them arguing?"

"No, but I didn't try to. I've heard others in the neighborhood say they argued a lot, but after she had her stroke, I thought he was pretty decent to her."

"What did he do that made you think that?"

"He'd wheel her around the block in her wheelchair when the weather was fine." She thought for a moment. "Sometimes I'd see them laughing together out in the yard. She loved him, hated him, doted on him, and abused him. To her he was her brother Michael reborn, but with even more faults."

"Before his sickness, did Michael have faults?"

"He was both a chaser and a drinker. Jesse inherited a lot of his problems, and that's all he inherited."

"Did you ever see Jesse abuse Ruth physically?"

"No. I never saw or even heard of him doing that. And you can hear almost anything around this town."

"Did you, at any time recently, see any stranger or group of strangers around the neighborhood, maybe watching the DeAlter place?"

"People would come and look at it lots. It's on a couple of walking tours the historical society gives out to tourists. I've seen people sketching it and taking photos of it." She looked across the street and scowled. "Lord knows why. It's an ugly, ugly place. I like mine better. But I've only got eight rooms and I don't need a quarter block to put them on."

"I like yours better also," I said.

She smiled.

"How about strangers who'd come more than once. Or anyone watching after dark?"

"I know nothing about that." She shook her head, dismissing my question. "If Ruth DeAlter had let herself brood on it, she'd have been a most lonely woman. Instead she drank until her health vanished. Everyone close to her was gone except Jesse. Dead and gone." She gave me a sharp look. "You keep shifting from leg to leg. It's cold out here and you're cold, aren't you, Mr. Fort?"

My legs were cramping some in the wind, but I was not that cold. I shook my head. "I'm okay."

"I'd like to invite you in, but that wouldn't be wise, not in these crazy days." She looked back across the street at the mansion. She rubbed her hands together as if to warm them.

"I can remember that house being ablaze with party

lights. There was Ruth and Michael and there were Michael's wives, one at a time, and the two boys. Now Michael's gone and the wives gone, all dead. Jesse's half brother is gone in Vietnam, and Ruth has been murdered."

"Jesse's half brother was killed in Vietnam?"

"Yes. He fell out with Ruth after Michael began to get strange and later died. Peter joined the army and I remember reading in the local paper how he got killed or lost in that silly war. Then the child Ruth favored kills her."

"Is *alleged* to have killed her," I said softly.

She nodded, brushing what I said away, satisfied with her own pronouncement. "Jesse was the second wife's son. Peter was a child of the first wife, not Michael's blood some said. Michael adopted him after the first wife died. Others here in town said he was Michael's bastard already. Peter went off to war and Jesse, when he got old enough for the draft, headed for Canada. He went to some school up in Toronto and stayed away from Scannelsville for years. Maybe he did it to get away from this town as much as the war."

"Was Michael violent at times?"

She shrugged. "Not that I ever saw. Just lost. Maybe it was Alzheimer's before they knew what it was. Senile." She stopped and looked once more at the DeAlter place. "Jesse was never a coward for all the town stories. He was very much like Peter, but years younger. Both of them were brash, abrasive, strong, and confident boys. Nasty at times when they were growing up."

"In what ways?"

"Both of them were sneaky window-peepers and petty thieves. They'd do mean things, shoot at birds and cats.

They had loud, fast cars when they got older. They'd fight some and sometimes the two of them would fight other boys. And noise all the time. They'd wait until after dark to do most of their mischief. Bright, intelligent, twisted boys."

I waited for more, but she pursed her lips and shook her head. "You've got your work cut out for you, young man. That Jesse's something else. A lot of people get better as they get older. My guess is Jesse's one of the ones who'll only get worse. He treated his wife like a slave and lived off her when he wasn't mooching off Ruth."

I could tell she was growing weary of me for now and I wanted to save her for later, hoping there might be more.

"Might I come back another time when there's more chance to talk and when I have more intelligent questions to ask?"

"Maybe. Sometimes I like to talk, sometimes I don't. Right now I'm tired and I've got more work I need to do before winter comes." She stooped down and pulled at a mass of dried mums. "You go on now."

"Yes, ma'am." I turned away. Outside the gate I let myself shiver openly. It was already cold to me. I thought about Florida or South Texas. The climate would probably benefit my legs. *But I have promises to keep.*

I moved on.

I tried other houses in the neighborhood without learning anything new. Some neighbors had witnessed arguments between Jesse and Ruth. No one had ever seen any physical violence from Jesse to her. No one had seen anything suspicious after the stroke. They had observed Jesse pushing her in the wheelchair and she'd seemed to enjoy that, sleepily smiling, appearing vague about what was going on around her as she rode. Some neighbors guessed intoxication, others thought she might have been under the influence of drugs, prescribed or unprescribed.

I kept doggedly at it until lunchtime. The last neighbor lady I talked with claimed she'd seen them screaming at each other in the side yard of the house and seen Ruth slap Jesse two years back. That was interesting, but didn't much excite me. I figured self-defense wasn't of that much value where the murder victim, if she was that, rode in a wheelchair on her best days, had a bad heart, and was recovering from a stroke.

I gave up at noon and walked uptown to eat. I had a solitary lunch at a busy hamburger joint called Ollies. The sandwiches and accompanying fries were greasy, undoubtedly unhealthy, and tasted great. I was back to the office by one.

Abe awaited me. "Karen DeAlter would like you to call her when you get in," he said. "She's called twice." He watched me. "How goes it?"

"Nothing much so far. I could've probably done as well picking at you some more. Tell me what you know about Mad Michael and Peter."

"They share an experience we don't. They're both dead," he said without smiling.

"Yes. Tell me what you know about them."

"Later maybe. Let me dredge things around in my head." He gave me a solemn look. "I heard earlier at the courthouse that Al, wasting no time, has the grand jury primed to indict Jesse as soon as Al's office gets the necessary papers typed. Murder."

"Separate page death penalty?"

"I didn't hear that. I probably would have if it was in the

picture. Maybe Al will try to use the death penalty for a
bargaining chip. Either you plead Jesse or Al adds it."

"Could be. Maybe he can get the job done on the murder charge, maybe not, but I looked the death penalty
statute over and I see no way he can ask for it—unless
there's a lot I don't know."

"At times Al can get fictitious," Abe said. "I happened
to read the statute myself again this morning and I agree
it doesn't look like it's in the case, but maybe Al doesn't.
He's got a lot of belief in himself and he can be a sticky son
of a bitch."

I thought of something else. "Peter, Jesse's half brother,
is supposed to have died in Vietnam. What would be the
quickest way of finding out for sure?"

"I could call the congressman. I know him. I could ask
him to get one of his staff members to check it out at the
Pentagon and then wire us about it. I seen it in the paper,
but you know them." Abe had little use for the local paper.

"Would you do that?"

"Sure," he said happily.

Fran came in the front door and hung her coat up. She
took her station behind the typewriter. She smiled her
juvenile smile at both of us, braces shining.

"I hear around we're in a murder case. I got asked lots
of questions about both the murder and you guys this
noon."

I smiled at her. News travels in a direct line in a small
town.

"What did you hear?" I asked.

"All the girls at lunch knew more about it than I did.
One of them who works for the prosecutor asked me why
you came down here from Chicago, Mr. Fort. Kind of like

she'd heard something about it. I said I didn't know. If I'm asked again, what should I say?"

"Say you don't know, Frannie."

She nodded, not liking my answer, and reached for a stack of papers. She was a thin, small girl, not yet twenty years old, and nosy as a two-year-old. She was good at the job. She chose something out of the stack and sat at her typewriter going at flank speed, ignoring us. She had little use for either of us, but she was better with Abe than me, perhaps because he signed her paychecks. Both of us were "old men" to her. She dated an unambitious county lad into raising tobacco and driving overpowered cars.

I went into my office and Abe followed behind. I called the number Karen DeAlter had left. The phone rang once and then was picked up.

"Mrs. DeAlter?"

"Thank you for calling me back, Mr. Fort. I went in to see Jesse this morning. He said you'd also been in to talk to him. While I was there, this one deputy told me that the grand jury had already indicted Jesse for murder and all that was holding things up was the paperwork. Jesse wanted me to contact lawyers in this state and in Kentucky who specialize in murder trials, someone who'd know special stuff about defending a murder."

"I told him that was agreeable with me."

"He gave me some names he'd picked up in jail. I've called two of the names he gave me. Both want a lot of money up front, lots more than I have or can raise. If I get someone, do you have any objection to staying and helping Jesse for now, then maybe being local counsel for whoever I get?" She paused for a moment. "Particularly should I get someone to come in from out of state?"

"No objection."

She sighed in relief. "I think you and your partner could defend him just as well as someone he'll have to give lots of money to defend him."

"Thanks for your confidence. Some lawyers who specialize are very good at it. But what money is Jesse offering them?" I asked. "Did he tell you I informed him that his aunt might not have left him anything at all in her will and that, even if she did, he might not be able to inherit it under our state law?"

"No. I do know there's got to be lots of money in his aunt's estate."

"But do you know if she left all or any of it to him? Has Jesse seen her will?"

"He didn't say he had."

"Some of the neighbors down around Ruth's place say she and Jesse argued and fought. You should realize that Ruth may have executed a will that cuts Jesse off. Then there's also an inheritance problem if he's convicted of killing her like I said."

Her voice was distressed. "Jesse says he didn't kill her and I believe him. That was family money."

"It was also *her* money. Before you place any more calls and excite a bunch of high-powered lawyers, maybe we should see what the will says, assuming there is one." From what I'd seen so far, there had to be a will.

"Can you check for us?"

"Come to the office and we'll look into it."

"Yes," she said. "But I have to go to work at six tonight."

"It won't take long if a will's been probated."

"I'll be along in a few minutes."

Abe nodded when I rehung the phone. "Let me call Nida at the probate commissioner's office and find out if there's a will probated or whether it was an intestate

estate that was opened. If there's a will, I'll have her make us copies of whatever's in the file. I heard in the courthouse that Al Windham's firm has the estate and that means there has to be a will."

"Perfect," I said. "If Al probated the will and has the estate, do you think we could call him as a witness and suspect on account of the fee?"

Abe grinned and went back to his own office. I heard him on the phone back there. The walls of our ground-floor office are thin plasterboard and you can hear right through them, which helps us keep up on each other's business. Once I slipped on a wet floor and fell against my wall and dented it enough so that we had to have that section replaced. *Classy*.

I remembered my office in Chicago had been paneled in oak. I thought about that and then didn't think about it, not missing Chicago at all.

Abe came back to my door and gave me the directions I was already expecting from listening to his call.

"Go over to Nida's. There's a will on file. And while you're gone, I'll call the congressman about Peter DeAlter."

"And does Al Windham's firm have the estate?"

"Yep. Big estate, nice fee. Nida is making you a copy of the will plus copies of whatever else is in the estate file."

"I'll be right back then. Entertain Karen DeAlter if she arrives before I return. Treat her just as I would."

He blushed.

I put on my coat and hurried to the courthouse. There Nida furnished me with a bulky document and a thinner packet of ancillary papers. I then hustled back. Karen had not yet arrived.

Abe said, "I got the congressman. He'll have someone

in his office check on Peter DeAlter. I had his birth date in an old file. With that they think they can get his service serial number."

"Great," I said.

We looked over the will together. It was only about a month old and it was long and complicated. It had been prepared by Al Windham and he was one of the witnesses.

The will left specific bequests to the local Methodist church and to Scannelsville High School. There was one sizeable trust established, money to be split between the local boys club and the Girl Scouts. It then left half a million, tax free, to each of the two servants. It left bequests to the Indiana University chapter of Kappa Alpha Theta and the Scannelsville chapter of Tri Kappa. It left pages full of small gifts to various local and national organizations. Here and there relatives were mentioned. None got more than a pittance. A residuary clause split what was left into two equal parts. Half went to the local historical society, the other half to what seemed to be an already established trust, the Ruth DeAlter Fund, overseen by the local big bank, income to be used for civic improvements within the city limits of Scannelsville.

Jesse DeAlter's bequest was in the will. He got more than any other relative remembered therein. He was left ten thousand dollars.

The other witness to the will was one Thomas Yearlin. I knew him. He was my local doctor.

Abe smiled with admiration. "Ruth was making certain no one could make the claim she wasn't of sound mind when she signed her will. Makes you wonder, doesn't it?"

"About what?"

"Her relationship with Jesse. She must have hated lots

not to leave him substantial money when she knew that was all he'd ever wanted from her."

"I suppose that's true. A love-hate relationship. Jesse hated Ruth, but loved her money. Ruth loved her money, but hated Jesse."

We looked over the other papers in the file. There was a petition for probate naming the big bank as executor, estimating the value of personal property at six million dollars. Beyond that, I thought, there'd be other things, the mine properties, the mansion, and whatever other real estate Ruth owned. Maybe seven or eight million. I did a little quick figuring and came up with what fees the bank and the attorney could and would charge. I guessed a quarter of a million each, maybe more. I knew Al and his firm didn't work cheap. It was enough of a fee for both bank and Al to wish for a client's demise.

I heard someone enter the waiting room and I went out. Karen DeAlter was there in crisp nurse whites. She hung a dark raincoat on the halltree.

"It's trying to snow," she said.

I took her into my office and handed her the will and ancillary papers. I went out into the waiting room with Abe and we silently watched Fran type. When I got tired of that, I went to the window and Abe went to his own office.

I watched light snow falling outside, not sticking. After a while at that, I thought it was time and I went back into my office and watched Karen some more and waited.

When Karen was done reading, she laid the papers carefully back on my desk. "Looks like you people are all there is. All that money Jesse schemed and postured and planned for, and he only gets ten thousand dollars."

"Yes. You'd best go over to the jail and tell him the news. Will they let you in to see him again?"

She smiled confidently. "There's a deputy over there who said he'd get me in any time I wanted. I'm sure he has plans for some sort of repayment, but there won't be any."

"Is that the deputy who hates Jesse?"

"Probably. He went to grade school with him."

"You go over then. Jesse may already have said too much about her money and it could come back to haunt us up the line. Tell him to say no more. And don't take the will to show him. Tell him quietly. Then come back here."

She nodded. "Old bitch," she said coldly.

We went back into my office when she returned. I could almost feel Abe straining to listen through the thin walls.

"How'd he take it?" I asked.

"Not bad. He laughed. Maybe he expected it." She made a tiny grimace. "He wanted me to kiss him before I left. It irritated him when I didn't let him—more than the money."

"Maybe your reaction was wrong," I said.

"You handle his legal problems and I'll take care of my relationship with him. We're divorced. It's even harder to make him believe it in jail than it was when he was outside." She gave me a twisted smile. "And it was hard then."

I moved on. "Do you know anyone who lives down in the neighborhood near Ruth's house?"

"I guess I'd know a few people." She thought for a moment. "I did special duty for Estelle Headley's husband. He died, but I got to know her pretty well. She lives right across the street."

"I know. I talked to her this morning," I said. "Do you

think she'd let you use a room in her house at night to watch the DeAlter place for a while—maybe a day or a week? Not today, but soon, when they close the house?"

"Probably. Why would I be watching the house?"

"Someone or some group of people might try to get inside it."

"I suppose I could ask and have my shift changed for a week. But I'd have to sleep sometime."

"I'd be there also most of the time."

"Why would we be doing this?"

I found and handed her one of the note copies that Judge Westley had received. She gave me an uncomprehending look after reading the note. "Where did you get this?"

"Someone anonymously mailed it to an official or officials in the courthouse. One of them made me a copy."

She accepted my answer without a change of expression. "Does this mean that someone was watching the house before or after Ruth was killed?"

"It came in the mail after Ruth was dead, but my guess is that whoever sent it is referring to a time before the fact. I'm not sure either way."

She looked down at her hands, thinking on it. Finally she looked back at me. "The two servants will leave the property when it's closed. You think that whoever is or was watching might then come back?"

"Possibly. Do you know if there's anything in the house of great value?"

"There are some antiques. But whoever is out there, if there's someone, would know those antiques would go at the sale and be taken by the buyer." She shook her head. "You're talking about afterward."

"Yes, afterward. If someone wants what's sold, they can

follow the buyer. I'd be interested if anyone did do that, but more interested if anyone tried to get into the house after it gets closed down. It's a long shot that it means anything, but it's better than nothing at all."

"There's the servants also," she said.

"What do you mean by that?"

"It says in the will they each get half a million, tax free. Jesse gets ten thousand."

"And so?"

"Why isn't the prosecutor looking at them?"

"Maybe he already has. Do you know the servants?"

"By sight. I was only in the house one time. That was when Jesse took me there to introduce me as his future wife. I wasn't long in the house that time. She asked me to leave and I obliged her."

I smiled at her look of anger. "We'll find out when the sale of real and personal property will be and try to figure out from that how long the servants will stay. After they leave, we'll keep watch. If nothing turns up, then we'll have a better look at the servants. I hear they were both with her for years."

Karen said, "And I hear it was never all sweetness and light."

"From Jesse?"

"Yes, Jesse."

"If Jesse had money, I'd hire someone else to do the watching. Without money, there's you and me and only so much time. That's assuming you want to help."

She gave me a long, hard look and then dropped her eyes. "Yes. You and me."

"Does that bother you?" I asked softly.

She looked quizzically at me. "Some. It wouldn't bother

me so much if you'd tell me where we've met before. I know we have met."

"Yes, we met. On a hospital ship a long time ago. South China Sea. My jet got a missile up its tail and I was burned some."

"Okay," she said. "I was thinking maybe that was when it was. I remember you. Your legs were bad. The doctors said you'd never walk again. The other nurses and I called you the quiet one. You didn't cry or scream, although we knew you hurt. You never demanded pain pills. Once, when you were asleep, just before they flew you off to Japan, I saw part of your face where the bandages had come loose." She involuntarily looked down toward where my legs were hidden by the desk.

They work, Karen.

"Why didn't you tell me yesterday?" she asked, watching me more closely.

"I don't know. I guess maybe I didn't want to remember bad times."

She reached a strong, slim hand and touched mine and I was burned again. I thought she knew it, but she kept her hand on mine anyway. "We'll watch," she said. "But watching and hiring you are the last things I owe him."

"Why do you believe you owe him anything at all?"

She shook her head, not knowing.

"Would he help you?"

"Jesse? God no. He'd run away. He'd get drunk or go to Canada or write a book. But I'm me, not him. Now tell me what you're doing about defending him?"

I grinned, wanting her to know. "Come tomorrow, I'm going to begin creating some chaos. I'm going to push and pick and make the prosecutor go to work. I'm going to file a fat claim for Jesse, if he'll sign one, on Auntie Ruth's estate. In the murder case, I'm going to file lots of hurry-up papers and then I'm going to do some looking for other suspects, like the servants." I thought for a moment. "One thing I'd like you to do for me is say nothing more about Ruth."

"Why? I hated her. What little there was to my marriage she did her best to destroy. My hate for her hasn't stopped because she's dead. To her I was that cheap little coalhole hussy who trapped her sweet, high-class Jesse."

"It's fine to feel that way about her, but just don't say it other than to me. I don't know exactly how they'll charge Jesse, but if poison or drugs gets into it, then the prosecutor might try to claim Jesse got what he's supposed to have used from you."

"That's silly. I wouldn't do anything like that. I'm a nurse." She shook her head, perhaps angry at me for telling her to hide her feelings.

"I believe you in what you say. But it will be better for Jesse and my case if you say nothing bad about Ruth from now on."

She nodded reluctantly.

I persuaded her to call Mrs. Headley from the office. She used my phone and I listened.

In the way women have, whether they're nine or ninety, they traveled intricate paths before they arrived at the business in which I had an interest. I listened while they discussed mutual friends, then their respective healths, and then Mrs. Headley's deceased husband, Horace.

Finally Karen got to the subject. "You know of course about Jesse?" She smiled conspiratorially at me and my pulse rate quickened.

"Well, we need to watch the DeAlter place from somewhere near it," she continued. "Not now, but soon, without anyone knowing we're secretly watching." She was silent and then she looked at me and nodded. "Could we? Oh, that would be grand and so nice of you." She paused again. "There'd just be me and Jesse's lawyer that the court appointed." She waited some more. I believed my pedigree was being discussed. "No, nothing like that. He seems good at his business and interested in helping Jesse." She held up her left hand and gave me a "V" for victory.

There was more woman talk, but finally she hung up.

"It's okay," she said. "There's a corner room and you can see two sides of the house from it. She'll let us watch from there. I left her thinking the whole thing would be an adventure for her."

"What did she say about me?" I asked. "I met her in her yard this morning."

"Not a lot. She said you seemed all right for a lawyer. She hasn't a lot of use for lawyers as a class. She wanted to know if you'd been ill. She thought you acted kind of cold-natured and said you walked funny. Are you okay?" she asked, smiling.

"Most times."

She looked down at her watch. "I'm keeping you from doing legal things. I'll go now and come back tomorrow? Will Jesse go to court then?"

"Possibly. I won't need and don't want you there if he does."

"Why?"

"Because I want you on the sidelines when I'm hurrying the prosecutor. He might think there was some advantage in it for him if he went after you. So you stay away."

"All right. Call me when you want me or when you want to go see Mrs. Headley's room."

"I'll do that."

She got up and I followed behind into the reception room and saw her out the door.

Fran sat silently behind her typewriter and refused to look at either of us until Karen was out the door. Earlier I'd seen her envious eyes on Karen.

I went back into my office and doodled notes on a yellow pad. I got out an estate claim from the form file and did my own typing on it. I was a fair typist, no Fran, but good enough and getting better. When the claim appeared to be finished, I then typed up a petition to let to bail, following the statute.

Fran came to my door at three o'clock. She stood there watching me type and I couldn't read her expression.

"I could have done that for you," she said hesitantly.

"I may put you to work in the morning redoing this stuff," I lied. I'd not dictated what I was working on to her because I thought there was a good chance it would be on the street before I was out of the office. I had no great belief in Fran's ability to keep her mouth closed.

Fran said, "She sure is good-looking for an older woman." She rolled her eyes expressively. "I mean she truly is real well preserved." She made it sound as if Karen could and should apply for social security. "You watch yourself with her," she finished darkly. "She's quicker on the track than you'll ever be and she's been around. I can see it."

"I'll watch her," I said, hiding my amusement.

I went back to my typing after I heard the front door close. For better or worse, I was about to be part of an upcoming small-town shoot-out where the reasons why a criminal case got filed weren't as important as who won it.

First, as soon as it was available, I wanted a copy of the indictment to see exactly how the state claimed Ruth DeAlter had died. I wanted then to hear tapes of the grand jury testimony. I also wanted to have a look at whatever the grand jury had seen in the way of exhibits.

I made myself a short list of reminders. I also needed a motion for a speedy trial and I'd done a rough copy. I needed discovery. I needed to know what else Jesse had done on the day he was alleged to have killed his aunt.

I thought about another thing, something I'd already warned Jesse partially about. Windham, from what I'd seen, was a plodding man, a loud, shrill voice, and an overpowering personality. But I didn't believe him to be very much in the brain area. I did believe he was someone who remembered where previous successes had come from, who redid what had gone well for him before. My defendant in the vehicular homicide case had told me he'd been watched while he was in jail. I'd heard from Abe that Windham liked to call county-jail prisoners and have them testify about what they'd observed in the jail. It had done him no good in my winning drunk driver case because my client had made early bond.

But this time, with Jesse in jail, I thought it was likely Al would try the gambit yet another time.

I decided not to be surprised, but to be prepared instead. Prisoners in jail, waiting to be tried or sentenced, serving out time, are easy people to get to testify for a possible favor, for days off, not promised but implied, for special treatment, extra cigarettes, visitation, food.

I'd serve him a witness list myself listing all the jail

prisoners. And maybe I'd even call some of them at the trial.

But first there'd be the petition to let to bail and a hearing on that . . .

I tinkered with that. An idea came to me. I remembered a man who was a special friend of mine, a bright, confused man who spent his days watching a puzzling world from the courthouse wall when he wasn't in jail, which oftentimes he was.

Bill Bottoms. *Silent Bill.* Deaf and dumb, but with a gift few knew of. He could read lips.

I got out a manila folder, assembled my notes and the typed papers I already had roughed out.

Sitting there it became difficult to keep my attention on business and my eyes wide open. I put the bulky will and the will documents in my file. I added my work notes and typed sheets and the two copies of the anonymous letter Judge Westley had given me.

I left the file open and tried reading the will once more, as if there was something in it I was missing which would help me. There was not. Ruth DeAlter had been thorough. She'd spelled out in detail exactly who, in each organization she'd left her money to, was to manage it, names, addresses, job title. I'd known of attorneys and executors having trouble where the will wasn't specific. But Ruth's seemed problem free.

One clause intrigued me. It read: "I have considered all my relatives, living, dead or missing and presumed dead, their families, and all of those who may say they were my friends. My failure to leave them a bequest in this, my last will, is intentional and not because they were forgotten or ignored." So much for Peter.

Checking him out seemed almost a waste of time. If he was alive and had somehow secretly returned to the Scannelsville area, there was no payoff for him in Ruth's demise. But, of course, he could not have known that. At least until after she was dead and the will was probated.

There was always revenge.

Sometime soon I would look for a picture of him at the local library. They kept old high school annuals there in the genealogy room. I'd once seen a row of them when I'd visited the room with Abe.

I thought more and more sluggishly and finally I dozed.

My dream was a girl with royal blue eyes and of running perfectly, with her, down a brilliant white beach in some warm place, an unspoiled and deserted beach. Somehow I knew it was a dream because of the way I ran and also because there were no such beaches left.

Sometimes I could see her face and I thought it was Karen, but many times her face was hidden. We ran and ran . . .

Someone opening the outer door to the office awakened me.

I glanced down at my watch. Half past three. I wondered if I'd snored and Abe had heard. Sleeping during office hours was a great advertisement for a supposedly eager young lawyer. Too much extra Canadian the night before.

Abe liked for me to greet newcomers after Fran had left, so I got stiffly up. Meeting people, possible clients, was a part of his expressed plans for me and my future Scannelsville prospects.

There were three people in the outer office. They must have arrived at about the same time, but did not appear to be together.

I didn't recognize the man, but he nodded at me as if we were acquainted.

The other two arrivees were women, the same two I'd seen with Abe in the courtroom. They seated themselves as far away as possible from the man, huddled together, nodding and whispering. One of them, up close, was very old and as withered as a sun-dried raisin. She wore a hat with a thin veil. In a corner, near her and within easy reach, she'd leaned a pronged cane. Her right eye was white and dead. The other eye was alive and watched me curiously. I thought her to be one of those older people who'd never lost interest in the world around her.

The younger woman had a hard, attractive face. She was tall and well dressed in dull red wool. She smoked a thin, dark cigarette as if she needed it to exist. She smiled without meaning and exhaled strong smoke. The old woman, caught in the cloud, coughed loosely.

"Who's first?" I asked.

The man nodded tranquilly. "Do them first. I can wait. Used to it, I am."

"All right," I said, more curious about him than them, but willing to be guided.

The old woman looked at the floor and let the young one lead. I tried to compute ages. Maybe eightyish for the old lady, forty plus for the younger one.

"How may I help you?"

"You're Mr. Fort. We saw you in court the other day and read about you in a local newspaper. Mr. Sapenstein has been aiding us. We'd like to see him and perhaps you," the younger one said. She wore small, half-glasses, very stylish. Her manner was precise.

"Mr. Sapenstein is here and I'm certain can talk to you. If he needs me to help, he'll tell me."

She frowned a little at my lack of enthusiasm.

"I'll take you back to his office if you'll put out your cigarette. Mr. Sapenstein's allergic to them." So, for that matter, was I, ever since the flames.

"Of course." She put out a thin, strong hand and shook mine. "My name's Mildred Marsh. This is my great aunt, Mrs. Flynn. For our own reasons we've an interest in the history of Scannelsville. This whole town is built on and over coal. Some of the people who first came here were from the Pennsylvania coal families that were our ancestors." She ground out her dark cigarette in an ash stand and helped the older woman to a tottery stance. She got the three-pronged cane from the corner and placed it in the old woman's trembly right hand.

I led them back down the hall. Abe sat at his desk, watching the door.

"I heard," he said. "Hello again," he said to the women. "I wondered if you'd return."

It wasn't the first time someone had come to the office to see Abe about the history of Scannelsville. His father and his father's father before him had been local merchants and Abe had great interest in the history of the town. And Mildred Marsh sounded to me like the typical genealogy fanatic.

I shook my head vigorously from behind the women to show Abe my own disinterest after we'd seated them. I knew very little about the families who'd once controlled the area and run Cannell County. I knew only what Abe and others had disclosed in discussing the town at Pajama's or elsewhere. And, just now, I didn't need to know more about anything other than the DeAlter case.

I excused myself and went back to the waiting room.

The man who got up from the chair where he was slouched stood tall enough so we could look each other over. He held out a hand and I eyed it and then took it. It was about half again the size of mine, although he wasn't an inch taller than me. We shook. My own hands remained strong from the time when I'd not been sure about whether I'd walk again. Once I'd made them strong, I'd managed to keep them that way.

There was no contest. He massaged my hand firmly and looked me over, then let go. "Do you know who I am?"

"No."

"The name's James Murphy. They call me Murph or Murphy or James or Jim. Whatever. For the last half century I worked, first for Michael DeAlter, then for Ruth. I was in the house the night she died. Yesterday I did my talking to the grand jury and I got warned not to tell anyone what I said there and so I won't. But a friend in the courthouse told me that don't keep you from asking your own questions about that night and the time before or me from answering those questions."

"Chicken Abelard?"

He smiled. "I've known Chicken for a long time."

"Do you know anything about how Ruth DeAlter died?"

"Some. Jesse found her. He was in and out of the house earlier, I don't remember the exact time. I saw him outside talking with a black man on the sidewalk. Later I saw him out there with a couple of other men. He come in and went up to his own room and I heard him moving around up there."

"Was he intoxicated?"

"I couldn't say yes or no. I didn't smell anything, but I had a cold or my allergies were kicking up that night and bothering me. First thing that happens is my smell goes. Jesse, he come down to where I was, to my room. He wasn't real excited, but he come fast. He said she was all twisted around in her bed and on her stomach and he couldn't wake her. I went with him and looked and we called the emergency squad and they took her. I knew when I looked she was dead."

"How did you know?"

"She looked real different. Her face was dark, her hands clenched, her eyes open. There was some kind of mark she'd made on the bed with a pen the emergency crew found there."

"What kind of mark?"

"Like she'd had the pen out and in her hand when it happened. A squiggle. And they found a pen in the bed."

I'd not heard that before and I was interested. "Could you draw what it looked like for me?"

"I don't remember that good."

"Who else was in the house that night?"

"Annie was there. She's the maid and cook. Annie Tinker. I was in all night. Jesse, like I said, was in some and out some. Annie was out somewhere for a time, maybe having a drop of Irish. She likes her drinks. She hangs out down at that bar Will's Coop with the independent miners and their cronies. She came in late, but it was before Jesse came to my room and we called the emergency number."

"Could someone else have gotten inside the house?"

He thought for a moment. "Probably. It's an old house. We usually keep the doors locked, but with Jesse in and out that night maybe they weren't. I never saw anyone or heard anyone, but with rugs and all, maybe I wouldn't have. I heard Jesse because his room ain't carpeted. It never occurred to me to check the house after the fact that night. Never occurred to them either."

"You mean the police?"

"That's right."

"What else did you hear that night?"

"I don't remember anything out of the way. I'm always hearing odd things in the house. It's got its ghosts. Things creak and pop. Big, drafty old barn."

"Where is Jesse's room?"

"Next to hers. She liked to have him close so as to talk with. Sometimes, nights, she'd drift in and out of sleep unless she took pills. Sometimes not even pills would put her under. Old and sick and stubborn. But a grand lady."

"Did she take a lot of medicine?"

"Whatever she wanted to take. She was a difficult woman with everyone, doctors and lawyers included." He thought again. "Jesse said he'd been in his own room and had gone over to hers to check her because he thought he heard her. He found her like she was, already dead, and we called the emergency ambulance."

"You said you'd seen Jesse outside talking or meeting with people? Did you ever see anyone else hanging about the house that night?"

"No. Just the people Jesse met."

"How about drugs? Was Jesse on anything at all when he came to your room?"

"I don't know for sure. He seemed okay."

"Why did Jesse stay with her? I mean, did she ever, in your presence, promise him money or tell he'd be paid or rewarded for taking care of her?"

"I never heard her say nothing like that. I guess Jesse came and stayed with her because his wife was always running him off."

"So Karen would run him off and he'd move in the room next to his aunt?"

"Yep." Murphy smiled. "She made a lot of wills also. She'd change her will and then change it again. She'd run through most of the local lawyers except maybe you. I seen a will once where she left almost everything to Jesse, but that was a while back, maybe four or five wills ago. The night she died, her latest will was there on the nightstand beside her."

"Next to her bed?" I asked, interested.

"Yeah. And the emergency boys, they found a pen under her body like I said."

I thought on that. *Maybe another change.*

Through Abe's adjoining wall, as I sat there thinking, I could hear low sounds of conversation and make out some words.

Murphy cocked his head, listening also. "Them women looked familiar."

"How so?"

He shrugged, not knowing.

"Jesse's half brother Peter, how well did you know him?"

"I knew him. He was a mean bastard. Michael got him out of half a dozen scrapes."

"Why exactly did Peter leave?"

"Michael caught him stealing stuff." He looked up at the ceiling, remembering. "Michael, he was a fine man, Mr. Fort. He made the DeAlter mare go, all of it, the house, the mines for a long time, the family, and the town. It almost killed him when he found out Peter was taking things, and Michael already a sick man. There was a row and Peter went away. Too bad. Peter was a combination of things, bright, mean, sneaky, talented. Six months after

Peter left, Michael was senile as a fence post, didn't know or recognize anyone. In a couple of years he was dead."

"And Ruth got his money?"

"No. In his will he left most of it to Jesse, having not forgiven Peter by the time it was made. But there wasn't much outside of the house and that was in joint title with Ruth."

"Was Ruth his executrix?" I asked, unwilling to give up.

"No. The bank."

"How did Michael die?"

"He was working on something. Even after he lost hold of his head, you could give him a piece of wood and he'd carve on it. If you gave him wood and stone or brick together, he'd put them together, cunning-like, one piece fitting into another. An engineer, that's what Michael was. They thought he might have fallen down the basement steps when he was supposed to have been in bed. No one heard it. He was a wanderer, alone and unknowing. They found him in the basement with his head broke up. The sheriff then got some interested, but there was nothing to show that he'd not just fallen and then crawled away and died. That left Ruth one sad woman, Mr. Fort. After Michael died, she was never the same. The only time I ever saw much to her afterward was when Jesse was around her and both of them high on whatever it was they were high on."

"Scotch?"

"Maybe. Maybe something else. I don't know and so I won't guess. Mine was a good job. I did it like it was supposed to be done and I didn't go sniffing into things to do it."

"You saw Ruth and how she died?"

"Yes. There was a big pillow on the floor beside her, not

over her face. She was on her stomach on the bed. There were pill bottles and her will on the nightstand."

"Who normally gave her medicine to her?"

"Sometimes no one. She'd get it herself. If she wasn't feeling well, she had a little bell on her night table and she'd ring it. Once was for Jesse, twice for Annie, three times for me. On that night, all I ever heard was the bell ring once."

"How many times did you hear it?"

"I heard it twice early in the evening. That was long before Jesse came to my room." He drummed a finger against his knee. "That big prosecutor asked me questions like he'd already made up his mind that Jesse was guilty. Me, I don't know."

"If I came past the house, would you let me see Ruth's room?"

"Maybe I could do that."

"And also where they found Michael?"

"That, too. But best be quick about it. There's the sale this week and then we'll all be moving on." He got up from his chair. "I'll be leaving now. You look things over and, if you get other questions, you come see me. And you can come and see the house anytime while I'm there unless someone in charge says no to it." He winked.

"Who'd do that?"

He shrugged, either not knowing or wanting to say.

We shook hands again at the front door. While we were shaking, I said, "She left you and the maid well off."

His hand tightened a little. "Yes. She did that in all her wills. I'm seventy-three years old, Mr. Fort. I was comfortable there in the house. I had a job I liked, a place to stay, and money in the bank. It was warm in the winter and there was plenty to eat." He let my hand go. "The money doesn't mean that much to me, even if I do get a nice chunk of it."

"How about Annie Tinker?"

He smiled and looked me in the eye. "You figure that one for yourself. Me, once the house is closed, I'll move out to my brother's on the Canaan Road. I'll hunt some and fish some and tinker with his farm machinery. But I won't have a real job."

"I thank you for coming in," I said, meaning it.

I watched him cross the street. He got into an aging shiny Cadillac and vanished down Main Street. I went back into my office and read the will one more time, trying to understand the old woman who'd put it together, trying hard to read her unreadable mind.

If Jesse had been in her room to kill her, wouldn't he have read her will? Once having read it, then his reason for killing her would have vanished unless it was anger.

I went restlessly out into the reception room again. The clock outside the building and loan a block away said it was a quarter to four. Chicken would still be in his office and the grand jury finished by now. There was time for a quick stop at the courthouse and then another at the jail.

I gathered my papers. Discovery petitions I could sign and proposed orders I'd leave to Fran in the morning. But I'd found out early in my practice that once a client signed something in rough he was less likely to change his mind and not sign the smooth. Claim forms were things I'd done before and I'd thrown all I knew about kitchen sinks into Jesse's. The petition for a speedy trial was rough and needed editing as was the petition to let to bail. I put them all in the file and went back to Abe's door. He, Mildred Marsh, and ancient Mrs. Flynn sat huddled together. Abe was drawing lines on a yellow pad, tracing family relationships. He smiled up at me, a man doing something he both knew well and liked doing.

"I'm on my way to the courthouse. See you later?" I asked.

He caught my meaning. "Of course," he said, visions of Pajama's Place shining out at me from his faded eyes. "After a while, Jack."

Mildred Marsh looked at me. "We could use your help here," she said coldly. "There are lots of things to run down in the library, even some famous old area cases to look up."

"I apologize for not helping, but I know so little about the town." I smiled at her. "Abe knows. And just now I'm very much involved in something else."

She looked back down at the yellow pad, dismissing me. "We read about that in the local paper. Some sort of nasty murder case involving one of the old families."

"Yes," I said. I moved on. If peace needed to be made, then Abe could make it.

The weather outside was now cold and dry. Rain had moved on east and I could see, as I looked down the side street, that the Ohio River was still falling. It smelled when it rose and it smelled when it fell, but they were different smells, neither of them pleasant or unpleasant.

I walked briskly to the courthouse. It was late. Most of the public servants had fled for the day. One or two assistants stared out at me from semideserted offices, willing me not to come in and bother them. The county council had turned down next-year raises in late August and mutiny brewed.

Chicken sat in his office, one big hand massaging his spreading bald spot.

"An interesting man came to see me," I said.

He nodded.

"If he's what the prosecutor hopes to make his case with, it isn't the best of cases."

"It wouldn't be the first time that bastard tried to start a stampede with a toy pony," Chicken said.

"Is the grand jury done?"

He nodded. "Maybe half an hour ago. They indicted your man for murder, but that was certain from the start." He thought for a moment. "One thing was peculiar. When they brought in the indictment, the prosecutor moved to dismiss the drug charge against Jesse. I ain't figured that one out yet, but the judge didn't act surprised."

I thought on the dismissal of the drug charge. Maybe Prosecutor Al didn't want anything complicating his case. A second thought came. Murphy had mentioned people outside on the sidewalk talking to Jesse the night Ruth had died. Was it possible that the two alleged crimes had taken place at about the same time on the same day and he didn't want to try to get a jury to believe that Jesse had coolly sold drugs to an undercover officer and then casually gone back into the mansion and murdered his auntie?

"What date does the indictment allege for the murder?"

Chicken held up a hand and said, "Wait."

I stood at his office door and watched a November fly fight the hot, naked light bulb that swung above the desk. The light kept winning.

Up here, on the third floor, I could smell the rot of the old courthouse. I'd read in the local paper that the commissioners were having work done and maybe it would include a new copper roof over the old building. I wasn't sure whether it was in time. The building smelled of time, decaying wood, old hates and sins, and strongly of the river three blocks down that rose and fell with the rain and the seasons.

Chicken returned. He handed me a machine-warm copy of the indictment. It charged that Jesse DeAlter on the nineteenth day of November did then and there unlawfully and knowingly kill Ruth DeAlter by forcefully placing a cloth or other covering object over the mouth and nose of Ruth DeAlter, thereby stopping the ability of Ruth DeAlter to breathe, thereby causing Ruth DeAlter to die, which death occurred in Cannell County, State of Indiana, the same being contrary to the form of the statute in such case made and provided. There was no death penalty page.

I looked in my file. The date was the same date Jesse had earlier been charged with selling cocaine to a state police officer.

Having the offenses charged on the same date meant something. It allowed me to have one witness I could call, at trial, to testify about what had happened for a part of the day/night Ruth had died. I smiled.

"It's confusing ain't it?" Chicken asked. "I'll talk to the judge about it tomorrow, but I'd bet he's already noticed." He looked out into the hall and then back to me. "If I know our fearless prosecutor, and Lord knows how I do know him, my bet is he'll be over here in the morning clamoring to push things along. An initial hearing would be first. It might be smart if you were also here. Nine in the A.M. Sharp."

"Advice accepted. And thank you for both it and the visit I enjoyed with Mr. Murphy."

"Murph? He's an old and dear friend."

We smiled at each other. *Allies.*

"Them papers you're carrying there in your file. You need to file any with the court tonight?"

"No. Tomorrow will be soon enough. There'll be more by then. Things to anger and frustrate our able prosecutor. Several of them."

"Fine, fine. Where now then?"

"To jail. I will talk to my client before the pot comes to a boil. And I need him to sign some of these papers in rough and agree to go along with my plans."

"And then to Pajama's Place?"

"Eventually and for but a short time. I'll undoubtedly need what's left of my wits about me tomorrow."

"Strong drink can be the ruination of a young lawyer, Jack," he said, grinning. He looked down at his hands. "I once was a regular until ulcers did me in. Say howdy to Killer Kilgore for me if he's still alive, and I hear he is." He nodded me on my way.

I added the indictment to my papers and walked from the courthouse to the jail.

Golden Lester Ballard, "Goldie" to all but the most heinous of criminals, smiled sweetly at me from a worn chair in his glassed-in office. A female officer dressed in sheriff's browns operated the radio. No other deputies were in sight. Goldie beckoned me into his private domain. He sat fatly in his chair and waited.

"I'm happy to see you so fully in charge," I said to Goldie. "I need to see my client."

"Wrong hours for visitation," he said.

"I never heard before that there're set hours for lawyer-client consultation."

"I just this day set such hours."

"Get him out here, Goldie. Or take me into the badlands of your jail to see him. Otherwise there'll be more of a smell around here than the one that comes off the river."

"I got orders," he answered, uncomfortable now, seeing he'd not easily faced me down.

"High sheriffs take no orders, Goldie. Within these walls they give them. No other official runs or is responsible for your jail. Just you."

I could see he was impressed by my words. He was a heavy, middle-aged man serving his first term, earnest and eager, and not stupid. He was a great handshaker with a lot of area relatives. He pushed his large gun and holster away from a place grown painful and his Adam's apple moved around while he tried to solve the problem of dealing with me.

"May I use your office phone?" I asked, still smiling.

"Who you goin' to call. You just yourself said I ran things in here. Ain't no one you can call can make me do what I don't want to do."

"True. But newspaper first, Judge Westley second."

He sighed gustily and gave up the fight in decent humor, and I wasn't sure at that moment that he'd not intended to give it up all along.

He got up from behind his desk and gave his gun belt one more wrench.

"I had a very bad night last night, Jack boy. Hit and run a couple of blocks from the library. Then the prosecutor climbed my butt because he said both my people and the locals messed up the hit and run scene." He looked heavenward for aid. "He said I could get back right with him if I kept you out of the cell area for a day or two." He winked broadly. "You know I tried."

"Who was the hit-run victim?" I asked.

"Old dude named Teeter Grimes. He was dead when we got there."

"What do you know about him?" Scannelsville wasn't that big a town and another death by violence was enough to excite my curiosity."

"Used to teach at the high school, but has been retired for maybe ten years. I guess he went to the library almost every night. Wandered around the rest of the time, late and early. Nosy bastard, but won't be anymore. Skull fracture, busted neck."

There seemed to be no reasonable hope of connection, but I was still interested.

"Could I have a copy of the report on it when it's done?"

"Done now," he said. "Why do you want it?"

"I'm not sure. Let's just say because there's another election coming next year. You might need me. So I'm selling out."

He nodded at my half-jest and half-promise and looked around to make sure we weren't observed. The female deputy at the radio was intent on trying to raise someone in a sheriff's car.

"Just don't tell the prosecutor. He sure don't like you, Jack. He wants your man bad. He's never done nothing like he was trying here to another lawyer."

"The feeling's mutual, Goldie."

He got keys from somewhere. "What I'm going to tell him if I have to is that I got ordered to open up for you." He stopped to give his next sentence emphasis. "By Judge Westley."

"What if he checks?"

"He won't. He's already started his run against Westley

and the judge knows it. Al will most probably win, too."
He rolled his eyes. "More's the pity, even if he is a member of my party."

"You do your best to make sure Al doesn't win," I said. "I'll help you get elected and you quietly help Westley. Think on it, Goldie. Al tries to tell you what to do and orders you around like you were his slave now. Think what it would be like if he was the judge."

He nodded as if convinced, but I had no trust in the nod. A political whore is a political whore.

"You got any reports or heard any city reports about anyone doing any burglaries down around where the DeAlter house is?"

"No. Not a thing."

"How about someone hanging around down there, maybe watching and waiting?"

"Just one undercover black state cop making a buy," he said. "From Jesse."

He led me into the jail. In weak light I saw two men sleeping in a tank cell, snoring loudly. I smelled the strong odor of alcohol over background scents of urine, decaying food, sweat, and dirt.

A thin, many-time loser I vaguely recognized but couldn't call by name recognized me or Goldie as we passed his cell. He started to say something, but Goldie held up a restraining hand.

"Your lawyer said he'd be over in the morning, Skinny. Talk to him, not me. And your lawyer ain't Jack Fort here. Jack represents the jail elite only." He grinned and we went on a short way.

Jesse DeAlter sat staring at the walls of his cell. He gave me a nod and waited for the sheriff to depart.

"Ring the door when you're done," Goldie said to me.

When he was gone, Jesse moved closer to the bars and my ears.

"I already know I was indicted, Mr. Lawyer. The sheriff read new stuff to me a little bit ago. And the prosecutor came along with him and wanted really strong to know what I had to say about it."

"What did you tell him?"

"To see you."

"The best answer. I got some stuff for you to sign. And I want to know anything you can tell me about your half brother, Peter. We're checking on him."

He gave me a mixed look, surprise and contempt. "He's long dead."

"Perhaps. Did you see him die?"

"Of course I didn't. And I never saw his body. I did see a telegram that Aunt Ruth mailed me when I was in Toronto. It said missing and presumed dead. I think there was a later telegram where they reported him dead. And I saw a newspaper story."

"Do you have any photos of him?"

"Dead or alive?" he asked, his eyebrows raised.

"Alive."

"Not anymore. Once, when she was heavy into booze, Aunt Ruth decided it was time to do away with the painful past. She burned all the old photo albums, school yearbooks, and whatever else she could find. She cleaned out my stuff and his. All she kept were her things and Michael's."

"Okay. I'll find one someplace."

He waited.

I thought of something else. "Did you know a Teeter Grimes?"

"Yes. He taught math years ago at the high school. I

heard in here someone ran over him. Stupid old piece of manure. He roamed all over town, nose into everything. Some people claimed he window-peeped."

"Was he teaching when Peter was in high school?"

"I think so." He waved a hand to change the subject, irritated with both me and his present situation. "I guess you're it—my very own personal lawyer. Karen told me there isn't any decent money in the will for me. I can visualize a cemetery full of DeAlters, including my fuzzy-headed father, spinning in their graves, but that doesn't get me any of the money. Somehow that old bitch stole what was mine and Peter's from our father, ran Peter off to die in Vietnam, and then cut me off in her will." He looked me over. From his expression I was badly wanting.

I waited.

"So what's your strategy?"

"I've these papers I'd like you to sign. These are rough copies, so there'll be others later." I handed him the sheaf I'd brought. I leaned back against the outer wall of the jail while he read them. I was tired and getting more tired.

Once he looked over at me and chuckled. A few times he nodded his head.

"Do they have to give us this bond hearing?" he asked.

"Sure do."

"You're sneaky, Fort. Did I or did I not do all this work you claim I did for Aunt Ruth?"

"If you didn't do it or something like it, then mark it out and then sign the claim," I said innocently.

He smiled, shaking his head ruefully. "You're sneaky," he said again.

"And so?"

"Got a pen?"

I supplied one and watched while he signed all the papers I needed.

"I'll bring corrected copies around, probably in the morning. Be prepared to go to court tomorrow."

"Sure. I didn't suffocate the old bag," he said to himself. "I spent the evening around the house. I had a few pops of scotch and I did some small, illegal business with that black guy who turned out to be a state cop. Del and Chester whistled for me and wanted me to go with them."

"Clarksons?"

"Yes. I stayed at home. Annie was out and it was my night in the barrel with Aunt Ruth. I slept. I woke up and went in to check her. I found her sprawled dead, face down, covers kicked off or pulled off, pillow on the floor. She was cool and getting cooler. There was a blue-backed document on the nightstand, but I didn't touch it. If I'd known what it was, I might have torn it up."

"There'd be other copies."

"I guess."

"How about a phone? Was there a phone in her room?"

"No. We took her phone messages to her. She told us what to say and we'd call back."

"All right. What you're saying is what we'll try to show in the bond hearing. A couple of cautions. She's not an old bag, she's your 'dear old auntie.' You had your spats, but she was your last blood kin on this earth unless Peter's lurking somewhere. You're upset because she didn't leave you much in her will, but you think your claim will take care of that. And even if you get a lot of her money by winning your claim, you intend a large part of it to go to this town and the area she loved."

He caught my message. "Yes. It was *her* money. What-ever she wanted to do with it, after I'm reasonably paid for the care and time I gave her, is fine. And I know and approve the fact that she left some of her money to a lot of great local groups. I hope that money will help them and Scannelsville." He gave me a sour look. "Is that better?"

"It is. Have you said anything different than that?" I asked. "Especially in here?"

He thought on it for a moment. "Maybe. I've been a bit perturbed and I tend to run on at the mouth now and then." He inspected me, liking me better. "You walk like you got a cob or something. You okay?"

"I'm far from terminal."

"You a vet?"

I nodded reluctantly.

"How does it make you feel defending someone who bugged out for Canada?"

"It was that kind of war. There have been a lot of times I've wished I'd headed for Canada myself."

He reached a hand through the bars and attempted to mockingly pat my cheek, but I backed out of range. "You lie, lawyer. You say Canada, but you did Vietnam. I talk Vietnam, but I did Canada. Life's a joke." He gave me his best white-toothed grin.

In a nearby cell I noticed the prisoner the sheriff had called Skinny lean our way as far as he could lean, listening hard. I stared at him and remembered where I'd first seen him—in county court on a minor theft. He saw me watching him and he vanished from view. I moved back close to Jesse's cage.

"In the last few weeks of Ruth's life, did you see anyone hanging close around the house, night or day?" I asked, keeping my voice low.

"The family ruins? Small chance. The only people in and around the house much were workmen. They were perpetually there to fix all the things gone wrong and keep us going. There were droves of doctors and her fat lawyer who's now after my poor old butt."

"No one else?"

He gave me a careful look. "Could have been and me not have noticed. Mostly I ate and slept there. On the servants' days off I'd wind up having to look after my aunt all day. And I watched her at nights and listened for her bell."

"Tell me about the servants."

"Exactly what do you want to know about them?"

"They both are getting hefty bequests in her last will. Could either or both of them have plotted and done your aunt in?"

"Maybe. I never saw anything. I got along okay with Murph and not so well with Annie Tinker." He shook his head. "She's a pistol, more a drunk than I'll ever be. You find out about them. Maybe my auntie didn't suffocate, maybe one or both of them killed her." He didn't sound like he believed it.

I waited.

"I can't help much," he said. "I'm in a box here."

I looked at him and he looked at the walls. We'd never be friends. He came from a world alien to me. He'd had a moneyed childhood, done what he wanted, evaded the war I'd fought in, and somehow gotten (for a time) the girl I'd dreamed of for years. Maybe he still had her. He was vain and pretty and bright and probably an addictive personality. A sociopath. A user of the world, uncaring about who he damaged.

I picked at his scabs. "What did you do for your aunt to get her to feed and clothe you and give you running-around money?"

His face went to full sour. "Nothing. I was just her sweet nephew who adored by her bedside."

I doubted it, but I nodded.

When I got outside the jail, I stood in the parking lot and thought about what to do. It was cold, but there was no wind.

Al had tried to make it difficult for me to see my client. That meant things might get tough elsewhere.

It was still late afternoon.

I felt eyes on me. I looked around, but saw no one.

I walked east on Main Street to the DeAlter mansion. I pushed open an iron gate with lions at the top. I walked up a well-kept walk to the front doors. There was a large brass knocker on the right door. It was bright with polish. I lifted it and let it fall twice.

Murphy came to the door.

"I hoped you'd be home," I said. "Things are moving along pretty quick and I wondered if you'd let me take a look inside?"

"Okay," he said. "Come on in. We got the place to ourselves. Annie went out for dinner." He smiled knowingly. "She should have about half of it drunk by now, the silly cow."

I went inside the huge double doors and looked around. The long hallway which bisected the downstairs was wide and carpeted in deep maroon. An old standing clock ticked loudly on the right side of the hall. There were doors to other rooms, some open, some shut. Halfway down the hall there were stairs.

"Follow me," Murphy said.

He led me up the stairs. At their top there was an even wider hall split by the stairs so that you could walk on either side of them back toward the front of the house. Murphy took the left side and I followed behind.

The room he led me into was very large. There was an oversized fireplace that was cold. The bed was a four-poster with a canopy and was neatly made. Beside the bed there was a large nightstand. I looked around the room. No telephone.

"Is it pretty much like it was the night she died?"

"I suppose," he said. "Annie has dusted and cleaned since."

I walked close to the bed. On the nightstand there was a silver bell. I picked it up and examined it. Someone had stuffed facial tissues into the bell so that the clapper was frozen.

Murphy smiled. "Blame that on Annie. She never liked the bell and now she's gotten even with it."

A large window looked out into the front yard and Main Street. There were two doors to the room, one being the door that we'd entered, the other a door that was open and where I could see a smaller room.

"Jesse's room," Murphy said.

I went to the door. There was a single bed, a small night table, and a lamp.

"Did she lock the hall door?"

"Now and then. Lately, with her being sick, it's been unlocked."

I walked back to the center of the big bedroom and stood there, fixing the rooms in my memory, sorry I'd not brought the office Polaroid.

"Would you like to see where they found Michael?" Murphy asked.

"Yes, please."

He led me out of the room and back down the steps. We

went through an immense, multi-mirrored dining room and then a large, modern kitchen. There was a door that opened downward. He flipped a switch and led me down narrow steps.

The basement was warm and dry. There was an empty wine rack on the east side. Beams ran up from a stone floor to the ceiling above and helped support the house. In the distance, lost from the light, I heard something humming electrically.

"He was over in the corner by the other doors that open to the outside," he said, pointing to an empty area. "The people who came guessed he'd fallen down the steps and then maybe crawled that far." Murphy shook his head sadly.

"Is it like it was then?" I asked.

"No. Since then they've put in a couple of new heat pumps, set them back on the stone floor back there." He pointed to where I'd heard the noise. "I put some concrete around them when they got to vibrating."

"I never saw a basement this big before," I said.

"The first mine was outside the house," Murphy said. "When the house got added to, Michael didn't want any structural problems, so he built it strong."

I followed behind and he led me to another door and unlatched it. Above, up steps, there were double doors that you could push up to exit. He pushed them up and the cold of the outside became a reality. The sun was almost down and it was growing dark.

We went up into the backyard.

"That was the old mine opening over there. When Michael closed it, he erected stones over the entrance to the shaft. He was a sentimental man, Michael was. That was where the family money started from and he wanted to preserve it. It's only been opened once since. That's when they were looking for money—when Michael died."

"Who looked?"

"Lots of people. People from the bank mostly, but there were some others. For a time I had to stand guard back here with a shotgun to keep them out of the shaft." He shook his head. "Nothing in there. I looked myself."

There was a fountain made of marble and brick nearer the house than the capped mine opening. A dainty maiden stood atop it watching where the water once had been, a stone girl.

"Who built the fountain?"

"Ruth. She liked to see the water falling, but when she took to her bed on the other side of the house, she told us to turn it off."

"I see."

He waited for another moment while I looked around.

"Is there anything else you'd want to see, Mr. Fort?" he asked.

"I guess not. Thank you for showing me." I walked to the mine entrance and inspected it. It was now forever closed by stone and concrete and I could see no signs of tampering.

I met Abe at Pajama's Place later. I'd been there a while before he came. I'd listened to the latest gossip, who was doing what to whom, who'd died, or was soon to die. I'd heard some old jokes. Everyone had treated me as usual and no one had yet mentioned the DeAlter family.

It kept getting later and I began to wonder if Abe would make it. Then, suddenly, without me seeing him enter the bar door, he was there.

He took a seat beside me at the bar. Doc Jacobsen, the

coroner, and one of his old buddies had the seats on the opposite side of Abe. I didn't much like Jacobsen. He was an internist who laughed too much and talked too much, but he and Abe had been friends down the long years and so I tolerated him.

"You must have been with a pretty woman to be this late," Jacobsen said. "Or making money."

"Business," Abe answered politely. "Legal business, Doc." He nodded at the waiting Killer Kilgore and received his Jack Daniels and branch water.

Outside it had begun to snow lightly, a flake now and then, no accumulation, just the pre-dust of what looked to be a bad winter to come.

Doc Jacobsen looked past Abe at me. "See you for a moment, Fort?"

I'd been sitting one stool away from him for an hour without talking to him, but I nodded. Jacobsen gestured curtly to the back of the bar and I followed behind him.

In the back of the bar it was dark. Some cases of empties were stacked against a wall. Doc leaned against them.

"What have you gotten Abe into?" he asked coldly.

"Lawyering, Doc. That's what he does and what I do."

"He's not that well."

"He was worse when I came. It was you who told me about a year back that you didn't give him six months until I came."

"An exaggeration. He gets to working too hard and I'll shorten the estimate. He has an insufficient heart. He ought to be packing for Florida now."

"Suggest it to him and I'll do my best to help."

He gave me an odd look. "What are you doing here with him, Fort? You came wandering in from Chicago and suddenly you're underfoot for him and me. Maybe you were good for Abe for a time. Now you're not. I hear bad rumors about you—that you got run out of Chicago—that you stole from a firm up there."

"Who gave you the rumors, Doc?" I asked.

He shrugged. "More than one person."

"Again, if you want Abe in Florida, you prescribe it and I'll try to help."

"No. I know that when there's a murder case and Abe can be involved, there'll be no Florida. And so you got yourself into a murder."

"I didn't ask for it. I got appointed." I looked him over. He was a couple of years younger than Abe. His color was bad and his hands shook. "How's your own health?"

"Tolerable."

"Wouldn't it improve and you maybe live longer if you quit practicing medicine right now and moved where it was warm and the only time your phone would ring, it would be someone for fishing or golf?"

"Maybe. I got me a job to do. I don't like Abe getting worked up asking me questions about that job."

"What did he get worked up over?"

"About the initial or whatever it was on the sheet."

"Tell me what you told him."

"No." He smiled coldly. "Let him tell you." He pushed past me and went on toward the men's room. I could hear him muttering about something all the way back. Something about me being responsible.

I went back to my stool.

"Dinner?" Abe asked.

"You, me, or Dutch?"

"On me tonight. The old lady broke loose and gave me five hundred dollars to do some research I'd like to do anyway." He smiled, thinking. "The younger one is handsome, but strange, with a mind that's very inquisitive about this town."

"The three of you seemed chummy when I was leaving the office."

I thought he tried to blush.

"Have you hopes there?" I asked playfully, thinking of Doc Jacobsen. Laughter is good medicine. Ask anyone, including *Reader's Digest.*

Abe smiled. "Old men dream the same dreams young men do, Jack. Old men's dreams come true less often. Sometimes, especially at night, I remember the girls of my youth. It's difficult for me to realize that many of them are now dust. I see them, awake or asleep, as they were sixty years ago, young and full of juice."

In that moment, as I watched him, he seemed as old and frail as he'd looked the first day I met him. I didn't much like Doc Jacobsen and believed him just about competent enough to prescribe aspirin for a headache and tinker with dead bodies, but I thought he was right about Abe. My problem was that there wasn't any way I could make him quit, send him on to Florida where he could play his bridge games and forget the DeAlters. Staying for the case could kill him.

"I apologize for anything I should apologize for," I said lightly.

"It ain't you, Jack. It's just that I know that the average age of my old girlfriends is now deceased." He changed the subject. "When you left, you were carrying papers and I heard you at the typewriter several times today. Tell all."

"I made up a claim in Ruth's estate for Jesse to sign. He did and I've notarized it. Plus a petition to let to bail and a motion for a speedy trial. I intend to push right on."

"For Jesse alone?" He looked me over. "Let me ask you some counterquestions about women. What are your plans concerning Karen DeAlter?"

"She's divorced from Jesse and some years over twenty-one."

"But after the divorce she lived with him, is willing to pay out her money to help him, and seems concerned. What bothers me with the both of you is what I see. You act as spooky as two squirrels in a storm when you get around each other."

His voice was low. Doc Jacobsen, returned to the seat on Abe's other side, had moved into a conversation about river fishing with two local merchants. I remembered what he'd said about an initial on a sheet, but it wasn't yet the time to pursue that.

Abe and I were about as private as things ever got at Pajama's.

Suddenly it seemed important to me that I sort it out. I said, "Karen's a handsome lady who married the local catch of the decade and then had it all turn worse than sour. She has her problems in letting go of that. I've no idea what their relationship would be if Jesse ever makes it outside jail again. So I'm trying not to complicate things more than they already are."

"You knew her before, didn't you?"

I nodded.

"I've watched her also. I think it will complicate whether you want it to or not."

"Perhaps."

He smiled. "Then let my answer be somewhat like yours. This woman is thirty-plus years younger than I am. There's something about her, something sad and secret, but she seems determined and earnest in her desire to

know about the Scannelsville of the past. She says it's for a
book, but I'm not sure of that. I told her I'd help her
where I could. Just now I showed her some things she'd
not already run down in the genealogy room of the library. I promised her we'd work on it a bit each day. She
wanted more, but I told her that I was in your case with
you and that it, being a criminal matter, must come first."

"Doc Jacobsen said something about an initial on a
sheet. What was that about?" I asked, thinking now was
the time.

"He said something to me also," Abe said. "I don't know
what it means yet, but I will."

"Okay. I want your help, whatever you have time for.
There are people you can help with, people you know and
understand better than I do." I thought about his new
female clients. "Does finding out about Scannelsville and
its history include any undue interest in the DeAlter family?" I asked.

"Nothing yet. There have been no questions about the
DeAlters. My bet is she's read the recent newspapers and
maybe Jesse's book. She'd done some research on her own
—or rather the two of them had—before some kind soul
touted them to me."

We got menus from Killer and in a while a buxom,
peroxided, locally famous waitress took our orders. Pajama's serves shrimp, chicken, good steaks, and a decent
variety of sandwiches.

"Let's steak it on my retainer," Abe said.

"Happily," I said. We each ordered another drink and
hand-carried the glasses back to a booth when it was ready
for us. The cloth napkins were clean and white, the uten-
sils were heavy silver. Around us, on the walls, lovely

ladies in various stages of dress and undress watched us
demurely.

"Tell me what you know about Ruth's live-in servants,"
I said when we were seated. "Murphy came to see me
today. Chicken had sent him over."

"Chicken has taken a big shine to you," Abe said. "It
started when you rubbed Al's nose in it during that vehicle homicide case you jury-tried. Murphy's full name is
James Lincoln Murphy. The woman's Anna Lynn Tinker,
"Annie" to friends and bartenders. Both worked for the
DeAlter family for a long time, years and years. I've heard
people say that Murphy once was a mean one and you've
seen he's as big as a house. He was a general handyman,
gardener, and chauffeur for Ruth when she was alive. I
know his family better than I know him. Irish who came
here to work the mines before the Civil War. His great
grandfather was second in command of the local company
during that war. His daddy worked the river—towboats. I
think I remember that someone died who was working
for Michael and Murphy got the job. Fifty years ago."

"He was friendly," I said. "He had nothing to say that
incriminated Jesse."

"Friendly is as friendly does. Al gets to hammering at
him as a witness and you might see things change."

"How about Annie Tinker?"

"She's got a drinking problem and she's had one for
years. I'll bet her liver looks like a shoe sole. When Ruth
got to drinking, it was Annie who encouraged it, kept her
supplied with Dewars by the case, and stood between
Ruth and people who tried to call a halt to the drinking. I
know one time a couple of years back. Sheriff Goldie
made a run down to the mansion after multiple com-
plaints and a report that Ruth was passed out in the ga-

zebo. Annie run him off. Got a mouth like a straight razor. Hangs around nights in tough bars."

"Maybe she has made some friends there," I said. "Friends who'd help her make half a million, taxes paid."

"I'm not the one to argue that with," Abe said.

The food came and we applied ourselves to it. Abe ketchuped all profusely and ate his french fries first.

"What will the two of them do now that Ruth's gone?" I asked.

"Move on. They'll have money."

"Will they move on together or separately?"

He ate the last french fry. "I've never heard anything like that, Jack. I heard, back the years, that when Ruth was younger, Murphy had eyes for her and maybe she had a yen for him. Whether anything ever went on I don't know. The town out there says yes, but the town says yes to any kind of dirt it hears. Murphy and Annie will go their separate ways when they leave Ruth's house. No love between them."

"Does Annie have family around here?"

"I don't think so. She came in from Louisville."

"At trial we'll handle James carefully," I said, planning it. "We might make him look possible there. But, in a petition to let to bail, we won't need to do that. If he'll testify as he talked in the office, it'll help. And I want to hear what he said to the grand jury."

"Could be one or both of them killed her," Abe said. "The problem for us is that Al has gotten Jesse indicted and he appears to be the best defendant available, the closest to the scene of the crime, the most likely. And, by the time we get to trial, Al will have his case. I doubt he cares, in the long run, if he convicts Jesse. He maybe just wants someone in jail, with elections coming next year.

And maybe he can lean a little more into the estate for a fee if he makes enough outraged noises."

"Well, I'd not want to stop him or any lawyer from making his fee."

Abe grinned. "A class decision."

"He doesn't like me and he's already setting up road-blocks for me," I said. I described what had happened at the jail.

"A pox on you, Jack Fort," Abe said, when I was done. "If he can hamper you, then maybe you'll do what he wants you to do. I've seen him operate for a number of years."

"And if I can shake him up, maybe he'll do what I want," I said.

"The will looks solid," Abe said, thinking. "You weren't going to try contesting it, were you?"

"No, but to make Al pause a little, I did get Jesse to sign a small claim on the estate."

"For how much?"

"Well, right now it's just an estimate, but the thought came to me that maybe Al might want to get a partial distribution or pay the named beneficiaries their bequests and maybe get some fees up front at the same time. So I put it in for eight million."

Abe grinned widely. "Al's going to be so damned mad at you he may lose his head completely and whomp you in open court."

I changed the subject. "Tell me what Doc Jacobsen said to you about Ruth."

"Not much. I guess there was a pen in the deathbed and some kind of ink scratching on Ruth's sheet. Doc told the prosecutor it looked like a 'J,' but now I got him unsure and am being careful to keep him that way. He's like a widow lady suffering hot flashes and hankerings at the same time."

Next morning, before nine, I was in the hall outside circuit court. Earlier I'd been at the office for some structural work on the papers I intended to file and then had taken the new papers past the jail for Jesse's signature. I'd also had, for breakfast, a cup of bad, strong coffee Chicken Abelard had supplied.

After I'd waited for a time, Al Windham breezed up, probably from county court one floor down.

He stopped in front of me in the hall and regarded me and the wall behind me without favoring either.

"You're the unlucky one representing Jesse DeAlter?" he asked. He smiled, apparently relishing the idea.

"That's me." I looked him over. He was an impressive physical specimen, taller than me by four or five inches. He also outweighed me maybe sixty pounds, a very large man, pushing forty, and now running a bit too fat. I'd heard it locally said that he sometimes dreamed publicly of being governor, U.S. senator, and even president. His next step up the line to the promised land was circuit judge. He was popular with area police and with the miners' unions, still strong in Scannelsville. His father had been a miner, one who'd died in a long-ago disaster.

I didn't know why the town liked him, but I recognized that it did. In my dealings with him he'd seemed contemptuous of the town, the rest of the area's political power structure, and the other members of the local bar. He was a king and Scannelsville and Cannel County were his kingdoms.

"You appointed or paid?" he asked.

"Yes," I answered vaguely and truthfully.

He ignored my answer with a head shake. "There's still some stuff to come back from the clinical pathologist. I'll give you whatever comes in due time. Autopsy stuff. Doc Jacobsen called in an expert, even though there's no doubt how she died. Jesse suffocated her. And the state toxicologist is working on stomach contents."

"Was she strangled?" I asked densely.

"No, suffocated. Jesse held a pillow over her nose and mouth until she died. She wasn't very strong, but she fought. I doubt Jesse had much trouble in overcoming her. Jesse's on the bubble with me. Maybe he lives, maybe he dies. You ought to tell him that."

I doubted there was any way he could turn the case into a death-penalty situation, but I said politely, "I see." I shifted my paperwork from one hand to the other, trying to decide when to serve it on him.

Not yet.

He watched me, his face relaxed and friendly, but his eyes not.

"Plenty of evidence to indict your pretty boy. And I'll get him." He looked down the hall and out a far window there, somehow restless. "I suppose there's a bare chance it could have been some kind of accident. Or mischance." He waited, his manner indicating I was supposed to get into further exploration of the subject.

"You mean you believe that her death might have been other than murder?"

"I mean I think Jesse might have accidentally killed her," he said evenly. "She was old and fragile and Jesse has bad habits. Maybe she read him her will and that plus drugs plus alcohol sent him over the brink and he accidentally killed her in the foray."

The idea sounded inviting and I wondered about it

being put forth. "It also means Jesse might not be guilty of anything."

He held up a hand and slowed me. "Only Jesse would know exactly what happened in his aunt's room that night. With you knowing his past history as a drug addict and a drunk, perhaps the thing for you to do as his counsel is to file something to get him examined by psychiatrists to determine both his addiction situation and the damage drugs and alcohol have done to him. We'd try to accommodate you and proceed slowly until all such avenues have been explored."

I thought on that. It seemed an easy way out for me. But promises and unwritten offers from someone I didn't really trust were worth little. An alternative came to me.

"First off, to see what happens with it, how about setting up a lie detector test for Jesse?" I asked. "He says he didn't do it."

"All of them say that," Al said. He shook his head. "You know how I feel about lie detectors. They're sometimes inaccurate and I've lost belief in them."

"You've used them before, Al. Why not now? They're a tool in situations like this one. Apparently you have some decent circumstantial evidence against my client, you have his proximity to the victim, you may have some bickering between them. Maybe you have more I don't yet know about. I've got a man who says he didn't do the deed. So why not a lie detector test?"

He shook his head.

I separated out one full set of pleadings and handed them to him. I waited while he put on a pair of glasses.

He held the papers away from him in one overlarge hand. "What's this? What is this?"

"Discovery. A copy of a claim we're filing in Jesse's

aunt's estate on his behalf. A motion for a speedy trial. And a petition to let to bail."

He was furious. "I talk sense to you and you serve me with a pile of crap."

"Talk sense about a lie detector and some of these things can become moot."

"Does your client want a lie detector?"

"Of course he does," I said confidently, not knowing.

"No," he said. "I guess the thing for me to do is add a page and seek the death penalty."

"Seek away. It should be interesting. I read the statute again yesterday. Adding it should bring joy to the world. What do you claim Jesse did, rob, rape, burglarize, kidnap, commit arson, or criminal deviate conduct?"

"Do it my way or get your nose rubbed in it," he said harshly.

"No."

"You're not helping your client," he said. He moved closer to me.

"Jesse signed the papers I've just served on you. He signed them both in rough yesterday and in clean this morning. He understands the risks of tampering with your political future."

His face reddened. "You snotty bastard." He brought up a hand unexpectedly and shoved me back against the hallway wall. I teetered. He stepped closer and I waited for him to get close enough.

At the far end of the hall I heard the elevator door open. Al stepped smoothly back, his face now set in a smile, seemingly friendly and relaxed.

"I intend for you to pay personally," he whispered, face smiling, eyes deadly.

"Up yours," I said.

The sheriff and a deputy brought Jesse in his chains and manacles down the hall. Al smiled warmly at the deputy and gave Sheriff Goldie a small, curt nod. The trio passed us and entered the courtroom and we were once more alone.

Al said, voice still low, "Don't mess with me or interfere in my plans, crip." He nodded confidently at me. "The way it's told they ran you out of Chicago. Now you've temporarily camped here, but this ain't the place for a horse apple like you. Move on. Other crazies, smarter and bigger than you, have tried to mess with me and my plans and been damned sorry." His finger dropped the papers I'd served on him to the floor and kicked them contemptuously with a huge foot. "No early trial date, no petition to let to bail. Discovery I'll give you. And I'll settle Jesse's claim for maybe a dime." He pointed his finger at me. "Play no more games with me."

He turned away and entered the courtroom.

I bent and picked up the papers he'd drop-kicked. I brushed them off as best I could. I followed him into the courtroom.

Inside the courtroom the deputy looked me over ominously and then let me take a seat next to Jesse DeAlter. Al sat across from me at the other counsel table. His face was serene.

I'd been warned.

We began. Initial hearings have taken the place of arraignments in my state. Jesse had gotten one for the drug charge when I'd been appointed. Today's would be another for murder.

Judge Westley looked down at Jesse. "Please state your full name for the record."

"Jesse Joseph DeAlter."

"And your age?"

"Thirty-nine."

"Where did you live at the time you were arrested?"

"With my Aunt Ruth here in Scannelsville. On Main Street."

"Are you now under the influence of alcohol or any drug which might affect your understanding of these proceedings?"

"No."

Westley plodded onward. He read Jesse the indictment against him, the statute under which he'd been charged and the penalty section. Minimum sentence was thirty years, maximum sixty. He read Jesse his constitutional rights about trial by jury, speedy trial, right to subpoena witnesses, right not to answer questions, right to be represented by counsel, and the rest. He then ordered Jesse held without bond and set an omnibus or pretrial date. All routine.

"Anything else, gentlemen?" Westley asked politely when he was done.

I stood. "I've some motions to file with the court. The first is for Mr. DeAlter to be let to bail. The second is for a speedy trial. A third is for discovery. The fourth has nothing to do with today's hearing, but I'd like the court to show it filed and that I served a copy of it on the prosecutor, who also, oddly enough, is representing the bank as attorney for the executor in the rather extensive estate of Mrs. Ruth DeAlter. Will the court let the record show I'm now serving copies of the motions and the claim upon Mr. Windham?"

"It may so show," Westley said watchfully.

Al Windham stood up at his counsel table. He frowned at me.

"My understanding was that these motions weren't to be filed today, Judge Westley. I've offered to open my files to the defendant's lawyer. My time, just now, won't allow me to engage in tomfoolery." He waited, very sure of himself and his power.

"I'll withdraw none of them," I said. I picked up the pile of copies the prosecutor had dropped on the hall floor. I took them to his table. The top paper had a shoe mark. I dropped it and the others on Al's table. Westley hid a smile.

In the back of the courtroom I saw a reporter for the local daily scribbling. A couple of other spectators also made notes, maybe reporters from the big papers in Evansville or Louisville.

"I could begin a hearing on your petition to let to bail as soon as tomorrow afternoon, Mr. Fort," the judge said, glancing at his calendar.

"I'm tied up in some civil matters then," Al said, doodling notes on a pad.

"Send one of your deputies then, Mr. Windham. We'll start tomorrow afternoon. And we'll decide on a trial date after we finish the petition to let to bail."

Al shook his head adamantly. "I want to personally represent the state in this matter."

"Two-fifteen tomorrow afternoon, Mr. Windham," the judge said, voice hardening.

"I need time to file an additional page asking for the death penalty."

"File whatever you want. But you *will* be ready, either personally or through your deputies, to start a hearing on the petition to let to bail at two-fifteen tomorrow afternoon."

Al gave a glance that smoked with hate and I smiled at him. I was still churning inside, but I hid it. No one had physically tried to push me around for a long time. If Al got close to me again, I was going to try to be ready.

Beside me my client Jesse DeAlter clinked his chains and gazed out on the world with what seemed to be amusement.

"It will take time to get the grand jury tapes transcribed," Al said, offering one more objection.

"Then I'll listen to them rather than read them," Judge Westley said. "And Mr. Fort also can listen to them." He nodded over at me. "Is that all right, Mr. Fort?"

"Of course," I said.

Al looked around the courtroom, perhaps counting the small crowd. He gave into the inevitable and smiled, making the best of it.

"Two-fifteen tomorrow then," he said, as if it had been his idea all the time.

I left undisputed possession of the courtroom to Al and the cluster of reporters who came to surround him. As I left I could hear Al talking loudly about the murder of the rich, bedridden victim, perhaps for my benefit. I followed Jesse and his entourage back to the jail. Once inside the walls, the sheriff and his deputies undid the irons, escorted Jesse back to his cell, and left us alone.

I issued one more direct warning to him to follow my earlier advice: "One of the prosecutor's best tricks is to get some prisoner from this jail to come to court and tell how you talked with him about murdering your aunt. So don't talk to anyone about anything, not even television, sports or sex. Read books, smile at the deputies, and cause no problems."

"Maybe it won't be that easy," Jesse said. "Couldn't he get someone in here to say I said something whether I did or not?"

"Perhaps. Let me worry about that. He's got some evidence. He's not in this barefoot, but we think there's a chance he's poorly shoed. What I want is for you not to help him."

"He seemed hostile to you in court."

"He's never been a close friend," I said.

He nodded and smiled and changed the subject. "How's the romance proceeding?"

I raised a polite eyebrow.

"Between you and my ex-wifey, who must still be thinking good thoughts about me, since she went to the trouble of hiring you."

"No romance, Jesse."

He nodded and smiled in a friendly fashion. "Maybe not yet, but there will be. I don't give a damn. Romance away. Get me out of this and I'll figure you're the chief Houdini of the legal world. I'll make Miss Coldpants disappear and you can see if you can make her reappear."

I left it at that.

I assumed that Al had yet to get much out of my client and now would be planning what could be done. That meant I should plan also.

In front of the courthouse, on fine days, there was always a gathering. Non-miners, non-farmers, and the area non-workers sat on benches and erroneously sorted through the problems of the town, state, and world. They whittled, they chewed, and they shared the stone benches. They told stories and split bottles of cheap whiskey and worse wine.

On this day, when I left the jail, it now seemed once again like early summer. Warm sun had dried the dead leaves and the very late November breeze blew gently. It was less than four weeks until Christmas, but for now, the wet and cold had gone into temporary hiding.

I spied the man I wanted to see. He sat apart from the crowd. He was, in truth, not a part of the wino crowd, although there was sometimes a strong thirst within him for alcohol.

I'd met my man through Abe, who only tolerated him. I liked him and he liked me. He'd noticed the way I walked and adopted me as a special friend.

At times he'd come to my office and we'd passed notes back and forth, me not knowing sign language. He was called "Silent Bill." His true name was William Bottoms. He was bright, thirtyish, well read, and interested in the world. He had one extra gift which I'd discovered, which he hid from the world and originally from me. I thought that gift could be of use to me now. He could read lips.

He was holding his notepad. It was yellow paper. He was doodling on it. He was a competent if uninspired artist. On the front page of the pad I could see the building and loan office across the street and the bar and barbershop beside it. The people on the sidewalk in front of the buildings were stick figures. The picture explained the way he thought on things. He inhabited an insular world in which he was careful of other people, but still he wanted to see and understand what he saw and read about.

He smiled up at me.

I pointed at the notebook. He looked around and saw

that no one was watching us and pointed at my face. I shook my head guardedly. He shrugged and gave me the yellow pad and I turned a page. Paper wasn't cheap and so I wrote small.

"Would you like to do a job for me that could be a little dangerous? For Pay?"

He read the question and nodded vigorously, becoming excited. He wrote in the book and then I wrote again.

As we wrote back and forth, he lost some of his enthusiasm. We sat for a time. The writing slowed. We eyed each other.

Finally he made up his mind. He nodded. We wrote back and forth again until I was sure he understood.

He thought he could get jailed easily.

Karen waited in the office. She sat across from Fran and they ignored each other. I beckoned Karen. She followed me into my office. I shut the door for what good it would do. I knew that Fran, if she wanted to be nosy, could hear us through the thin walls.

In the other office I could hear Abe moving around restlessly.

"I thought maybe you'd like to take a trip down to Mrs. Headley's house yet this morning and see the room she's going to let us use to watch the DeAlter house?"

"That would be all right. And, for your information, we start a bond hearing on Jesse tomorrow afternoon. I've also requested an early trial date and filed a claim on Ruth's estate."

"A claim?"

"A claim for services. If Jesse took care of her, he's entitled to be paid for it. It may not do us any good, but it and the other motions stirred things up in and out of court today."

"Your partner told me he'd learned the auction sale is tomorrow. That means, I guess, that they'll close the house down and the servants will move on. So the house will be empty by tomorrow or Friday."

"Did he say anything else?"

"No, except that you were in court and I remembered you said you didn't want me over there."

I waited.

"Everything seems to be moving so quickly," she continued. It didn't seem to completely please her.

"The judge was obliging. He gave us a very quick hearing on our petition to let to bail. The prosecutor didn't much like it." Or me, I almost added.

"Will getting bail set do any good. Jesse hasn't a dime and I can't make bail for him."

"The hearing will let us see what the prosecutor has, assuming he has something."

"I hear around that you and the prosecutor are enemies."

"That's true." I looked down at my desktop and then back at her. "I offered Jesse for a lie detector test. I figured that if Jesse didn't want or wouldn't take one, we could always back off. The prosecutor turned down my request. Polygraphs have fallen into some disrepute, but they've been used around here before and after that disrepute. It could be that Al refused because he doesn't want to make a deal on one and then have it come out not suiting him. A bond hearing should tell us a lot." I shook my head, remembering what Doc Jacobsen and Abe had told me about a marking on the sheets. "He's got something. I know that, but I don't know what it is. Maybe I'll know after I hear tapes of the grand jury testimony."

"Why would he be after Jesse?"

"Mr. Windham is most interested in moving up in politics. It wouldn't be the first time that a prosecutor has tried to ride a murder case to a higher office. Juicy murders are good for political ambitions. With Jesse in jail something good will come of it. Al can be a daily hero, lots of pictures in the papers, lots of interviews on area television. Now I'm in his way and I've made him unsure of any advantage by forcing up the pace so that there's little chance for helpful coverage. He was angry enough today to threaten adding a page asking for the death penalty for Jesse. That could be another problem for him if he tries it." I smiled at her and she smiled back appealingly.

"Legal maneuverings," I finished.

She looked at the picture of Abe Lincoln on my otherwise almost bare walls.

"Come with me," she said. "You're caught up in this and too nervous and intent. I'm taking you to lunch out in the country. If we eat together in town, people will talk, but I know a place miles from here that ought to be reasonably free of locals at lunch."

"How about this visit to Mrs. Headley's house?"

"That can wait until after the sale."

She drove her old Ford out a state highway that paralleled the river. She was an efficient driver in the occasional traffic, passing where there was room, content to stay in line when there was not. She was silent and intent about it. I watched her and let her watch the road.

Eventually she turned off the state road onto a county lane. It was crumbling blacktop, potholed deeply here and there, full of curves. The state highway we'd left had moved away from the river, but the new road ran back near the river's edge. On her side there were faded farm-houses and bleached barns. On my side, down below, not very far, the Ohio ran its timeless way, full of autumn drift, muddy from cannabalizing its own banks.

The sun on the roof made the car warm, but the fields were autumn brown. It would not be long until it was winter. Then spring and summer.

Life was short. Once mine had almost been terminated over a warm sea near a faraway land, but I'd survived. I now realized I was mortal, which is a hard thing for the young to understand.

I sat next to her, smelling her faint perfume and won-dering if she was mortal also. I knew she had to be, but I didn't have to believe it.

We passed an old, abandoned coal shaft, a big one. Karen slowed.

"My father worked that one half his life and then died there," she said without changing expression. "It be-longed to the DeAlters."

We moved away from the river. As we drove, I had the feeling I was being watched. It was strong enough so that I turned in the seat and looked behind us.

Nothing.

Around a curve there was a cluster of houses and a crossroad. There was one big house. An old painted sign out front read DINK'S PLACE. The big building, like the houses, was run-down, but someone had painted a bright coat of white paint on its front making it stand out like a scholar among dullards.

We parked and entered. After the sun it was dark in-side. A big woman came to Karen and cooed at her and hugged her, watching me curiously over Karen's shoulder.

She led us down a lighted hall and opened the door to a small room with a window opening to the harvested soy bean and corn fields and the nearby river. The fields seemed darker and richer than those I'd seen earlier, perhaps because of their occasional marriages to the river silt.

There was a table and four chairs. The napkins were red paper, the silverware worn stainless. Two menus were on the table.

"Are we still in Cannell County?" I asked.

"Barely. A hundred yards further up the road is the county line." She nodded at the menu. "Try the catfish."

I nodded and watched her. It was hard to find words, but I didn't feel uncomfortable.

"I'll take your advice. You've been here before and you know the people."

"Yes."

"With Jesse?"

She looked out the window toward the river. "Once. This place is owned by family. The lady who seated us is a second cousin. Her man died in a cave-in. My aunt's the cook. Her husband died four years back of black lung. The money from that helped pay off the mortgage." She smiled. "Buying it was a way to get the family out of the mines. I help out now and then. Sometimes, especially weekend nights, it gets busy and all of the rooms are full. There are some big party rooms and then there are other rooms like this for just a few. It makes them a living."

"Didn't Jesse like it?"

"He said he thought it was quaint," she said. "Jesse has a lot of words to describe things. I think maybe the place

didn't like him. Out here you can drink a beer or two or
sip a glass of wine or maybe a mixed drink before the food
comes. When it does come, you eat. That's what the place
was meant for. Jesse, he was a glutton for the drinking and
not that much for the rest. Elmer, he's my cousin who
runs the bar, had to help Jesse back to my car." She looked
me over. "They say that you drink, Jack."

"True," I admitted. "Too much now and then."

She nodded. "Would you like a drink now?"

"No. I have to go back to the office. I don't drink when
I'm working, but sometimes I drink after hours." I looked
at her and saw she doubted me, but what I really saw was
the reflection of my sun in her eyes.

We had the catfish. It was tender and juicy, farm-raised
rather than river-caught. The fillets were fried in deep fat
and had been dipped in some kind of thick corn batter.
There were fresh green beans and a saucer of slaw, home-
made muffins, and big tumblers of iced tea. I ate and
watched Karen eat. She ate like a hungry man, relishing
the good food.

"You could use five more pounds," I said critically.

She shook her head. "Most women always think they're
too fat. I'm one of them." She looked away, perhaps remembering an earlier time. "When you saw me on the
hospital ship, I guess I was a bit heavier?"

"Perfect."

"But not now?" she asked. She touched my hand with
one of hers.

"Now, too."

She grimaced. "I keep having the urge to confess to
you, Jack. There was a doctor on that ship and we worked
together. I found out very soon that he was married, but I
thought I was in love and we were both heroic and brave.

I quickly discovered that he was both vain and shallow. He was also a most practiced liar. So I asked for a transfer and, when my time was up, I left the Navy. Then came Jesse and, in his way, he was worse." She took her hand from mine and toyed with her iced tea glass. "They say women repeat their mistakes, Jack. If you divorce a drunk, then you'll marry another. If you rid yourself of a wife beater, another one worse will come to take his place and smile while he savages you."

"I'm not a drunk, although I drink some. And I'm not a wife beater," I said. "If you're asking."

She leaned forward, looked into my eyes, and then kissed me lightly on the nose. "I hope not."

I got up from my chair and pulled her to her feet. I kissed her for a long time, one single kiss. A little bit into it she responded, so that, at the end, we were both breathing hard. We were fitted together, her body against mine.

When it was done, she took her finger and traced my mouth with it. Her eyes had grown strange in the sunlight.

"I need someone, Jack. Maybe that someone is you. But not right now. I'm confused, recently divorced, and sometimes not certain why I got that divorce. I know Jesse can use the pair of us with clear heads and nothing in our way. Do you think we can do that for him?"

"Maybe."

"Try," she said. "I'm going to try also. I don't want to start up with you now."

I sat back down. I tried to understand both myself and Karen. And, underneath, I wondered if what she'd done wasn't just another part of an ongoing play, a play starring Jack and Jesse and other fools.

She pulled at my hand, looked at her watch and said, "Lunchtime is over."

That afternoon I made time and went to the courthouse and listened to selections from the tapes of testimony to the grand jury.

Chicken Abelard had taken charge of the tapes and he played them for me.

The tapes weren't long or particularly complicated. Some could be skipped because they were cumulative. After I'd heard one emergency technician, I could skip the others. After I'd heard the chief police investigator on the scene, I could skip the others. There was about eight hours of actual testimony, but it only took me about four hours to listen to it.

And I heard Al's most damning evidence. It came from Doc Jacobsen. He testified that Ruth had been suffocated and also that it was his opinion that she might have been given drugs or alcohol before her death. He also testified that after visiting the hospital he'd gone with the police back to Ruth's home. There, on her undersheet, he'd found a pen and a scribble on the sheet.

The scribble, Doc said, looked like a "J."

In addition to testimony from the police and the emergency crew, there was testimony from the servants.

The worst came from Annie Tinker. She talked incessantly and darkly of bad blood between Jesse and Ruth. She was more vague about threats of murder she'd heard Jesse mutter. James Murphy was neither good nor bad. The worst of his testimony was when he told of how Jesse had come coolly and unruffled to his room and asked him to go to Ruth's room because "something seemed to be wrong."

The servants described the layout of the house and also told the way Jesse's room adjoined his aunt's. They told of the other door to Ruth's room, but said it was normally kept closed, but not locked.

Both servants described Jesse's habits, his drug and drinking sprees, his minor and major thefts from the house, and Ruth's disintegrating attitude toward him.

I heard no testimony concerning the note that Judge Westley had given me and I wondered if it had been delivered to Al.

I sat and listened and listened, and then listened some more.

It came to me in the listening that something was wrong. None of the witnesses actually testified, but only answered leading questions put to them by Al Windham or one of his deputies, pushing along hard for an indictment.

"Now, Dr. Jacobsen, isn't it a true statement of the facts that you examined the body of the deceased woman, visited the room where she died, and found evidence indicating she was either drugged or given an excessive amount of alcohol and then suffocated?"

And "Officer, did you hear of any other person being in the vicinity of the room at or near the time of death of Ruth DeAlter other than Jesse DeAlter?"

And "Did you discover any other person with access to her room who had the good reason to murder Ruth DeAlter that Jesse had?"

And "Weren't Jesse's actions nervous and suspicious when you talked to him? Didn't he shake. Didn't he fail to meet your eyes?"

And finally, over and over, in questions to any witness who'd seen Jesse that night: "Did Jesse ever protest his innocence to you or was he too far gone to even care about what he'd done?"

It was kind of like the old story about asking someone when he'd quit beating his wife.

I made some notes. I never got to the place where I felt confident because there was evidence of a sort. Now and then I'd look at Chicken or he'd look at me. And also now and then I'd catch Chicken shaking his head, an old courtroom veteran who knew more than I'd ever know.

I used up afternoon and early evening in the listening. When the tapes were done, Chicken put them back into their holders.

"Lots of leading questions," he said.

A plan came to me. If Chicken saw the leading questions which led to inadmissible answers, wouldn't Judge Westley?

If the petition to let to bail was now heard and the prosecutor took the witnesses through the evidence again, one by one, then those witnesses had already heard the answers they were supposed to give. In such a fresh hearing most of them would say what he'd placed in their mouths before the grand jury.

I wondered if I could shorten the petition to let to bail by introducing or manipulating Al into introducing the transcript and then only go with new stuff, his and mine?

He'd seemed in a hurry. Maybe . . .

I looked up and was suddenly aware I'd kept Chicken after hours. I apologized.

"Not to worry," he said imperturbably.

I thought of another thing. "Chicken, the name on the information against Jesse for cocaine was T. Moss, ISP. Do you know trooper Moss?"

"I know 'em all, sonny. T. Moss is Ted Moss. He's a black

state policeman who lives up in Bloomington. He became a state trooper about the time I retired from the local department."

"Would he talk to me and be straight?"

"Maybe. I'd guess he would if he got told I'd sent you. He can't feel too good about his charge against Jesse being dismissed."

"Would you call him for me?"

"I guess I could. But your hearing starts tomorrow afternoon."

"I could drive up in the morning if he'd see me for a minute or two."

Chicken wet a finger and held it up against the air. "My knee tells me there's snow coming and soon now. But I'll call him for you. Tonight. If he can't talk to you, I'll call you at five in the A.M.

We went out of the courthouse together and into cold weather, thirty degrees down from the afternoon. We separated in the parking area.

By unspoken agreement between Abe and me, I decided I was supposed to appear at Pajama's Place and so I walked there, bent against a wind that had earlier been placid and now was severe.

"I don't care what he said before the grand jury, Doc don't know for sure exactly how Ruth died or who caused it. He's guessing." Abe sipped a tall, dark drink. His old eyes were faded in the bar light. "He didn't think I ought to be asking him more questions. He said you was the one to do it."

"But he did talk more to you?"

"Yep. After I deviled him some."

"He thinks you're working too hard."

"Is this kind of stuff work?" Abe asked, smiling.

"Tell me more about what he said."

Abe inspected his drink. "Al latched onto him outside the jury room and got him committed to a line of questions and answers. Al can be kind of overpowering, one on one. And Doc said Al asked him the kind of questions that were hard to answer, except yes or no. Doc said a few times he'd try to say more and Al or his deputy would hold up a hand and shush him. That won't show on the transcript, but he said that's how it was."

"Lord help the world to be safe from politically ambitious prosecutors."

Abe nodded. "Doc even went so far as to say that Ruth, in her condition, and having taken drugs and some booze, might have accidentally suffocated herself. Unlikely, but possible."

"She'd been drinking that much?"

"He said they found two empty bottles in her room. She could, using her walker, get around a little."

"I may just go with the transcript and a few other things in the bond hearing, but if it doesn't work that way and Doc gets called, could you take him on cross, him being your friend and not mine?"

"Sure," he said, smiling widely.

"What else did he tell you?"

"The rest ain't that good. He kind of diddled around, like the old maid he is, and said Ruth had been hanging on to life for months, ready to die, but fighting it. He told me, if it got down to deciding, he'd have to say that someone helped her along and that Jesse seemed both nervous and smiley about it at the hospital and spent a lot of his time talking about her good long life and that it must have been her time to go."

"We take what we can get. The tapes are full of questions supplying answers. If the same witnesses are called at the bail hearing, I'll raise hell every time Al tries that. We get sustained a few times before an audience of newsies and Al could get gun-shy."

"Or mad," Abe mused. "At both you and a judge with the knowledge Al wants to run against him." He drummed his fingers on the bar. "How about Annie Tinker, the newly rich maid?"

"She was Al's best. She said things about fights and arguments and threats."

I think he could tell I was getting restless.

"Anything else?"

"Don't look for me until tomorrow afternoon. I'm going to do some barhopping tonight and take a trip in the morning. And don't be surprised if we have a very short bond hearing."

Will's Coop was the name of the bar I'd heard about in connection with both the Clarksons, Jesse's friends, and Annie Tinker.

I walked there from Pajama's, a cold walk. The wind had come up and brought with it tiny crystals of ice that whipped against me.

It was a coal miner's bar. I entered and stood in the doorway.

In the far corner of the single, large room someone worked hard at an old, not quite in tune piano, playing and singing country into a microphone. There was a big, potbellied stove set off center, glowing red.

A few people in nearby booths looked up when I entered. No one seemed particularly interested in me and the watchers soon went back to their beer.

In a booth near the piano/singer I saw a lone woman, head down, leaned forward. Her face was wrinkled, her dress shabby.

I sat down at the bar.

The bartender looked familiar, but I couldn't place him.

"What are you doing in here, Fort?" he asked curiously.

"First off I'm having a Canadian on the rocks to warm me."

"That we can do." He smiled, exhibiting bad teeth and I suddenly recognized him as someone I'd met in the office. Abe represented him.

He poured generously until the cubes were covered.

"Is that Annie Tinker over near the piano man?"

He nodded.

"And are the Clarkson brothers around tonight?"

"As usual. In the corner booth on the other side of the room from Annie." He gave me a careful look. "I heard you was representing Jesse. Even so, I'd be careful of them Clarkson boys if I was you. Nasty. And Annie too. She's got herself a real mean mouth and I don't want no trouble in here."

"I won't make any."

"You just being in here and asking them questions could make it."

I stood and picked my glass up from the bar and he let me wander away without further objections.

I went to Annie Tinker's booth first.

"Could I sit down and talk with you for a minute?"

She looked me over. "What for?"

"My name's Jack Fort. The court appointed me to defend Jesse."

"I already said what I had to say in front of a jury."

"That was the prosecutor's jury. No matter. I'll just subpoena you and then you can come testify in open court and I can find out what I want to know there. And those questions won't be the questions you were asked by the prosecutor."

For a long moment she considered anger, but then she sighed. She took a sip of her drink.

"Sit down. Ask quick and then move on and leave me be."

I sat across from her. Despite the wrinkles in the dim light, she didn't look bad. Her hair was black, either from dye or naturally. She was thin and unbowed by years, an erect woman with good features and a narrow mouth.

"I have some information that someone or a group of someones was watching the DeAlter house. Did you ever see anyone watching?"

"People came past all the time."

"This would have been at an unusual time."

"I woke up one time a month or so back, lawyer. It was maybe midnight and some sound, maybe a truck going past, woke me. There was someone in the yard. I banged on my window and whoever it was took off running. I checked Jesse's room and he was in bed."

"You knew Peter DeAlter. Could it have been him?"

"He's deader than your pea brain," she said caustically.

"Did you see him die?"

"I ain't a Vietnamese vet, asshead. But Peter's dead and you can't resurrect him to help your client, pothead Jesse." She lifted her glass, frowned, and downed the rest of her drink. She banged her glass on the table and the bartender stopped polishing glasses and went to work building her another.

She was pretty far along, her body loose in the booth.

One shoe was off and I could see it by her foot. She lifted that foot and reached down absently to massage it.

"It helps more to wiggle your toes."

"Are you both a shyster and a quack?"

"No. I got my legs and feet hurt once. Try wiggling your toes. It'll hurt some when you begin, but then things will uncramp."

She opened her mouth to blast me, but then wiggled her toes instead.

"I'll be damned," she said. "It does help." She looked me over again. "You ain't as stupid as you look."

I nodded agreeably and waited.

"What else do you want to know?"

"Whatever you know. Anything that could help me defend Jesse."

She frowned. "There ain't a lot that can help him. They fought and argued all the time. He stole things out of her house. Things got funny on that. He'd steal something and I'd tell her. Lots of times she'd not seem to care. She'd just brush it off. But at the end, when she got crazy and mean, she did care. She'd raise hell with him and with me and Murphy. She was drinking some and he was getting her drugs."

"What kind of drugs?"

"I don't know. Little foil packets. I seen some of them. Maybe cocaine or speed or something psychedelic. Made her crazier than a deer at a high fence."

"What did you see?"

She lowered her head. "Nothing. She'd whisper to me that he'd got her something special. Maybe he was hoping she'd just die from too much of what she told him to get for her. She had bad arteries and a worse heart." She leaned toward me. "One time, when we was drinking together in here, I asked him what it was she was taking, but he just smiled." She looked at me with eyes faded from drink. "Jesse's a bastard of a man. He's pretty and people do what he says. He thinks he's better and smarter than the rest of us."

"Is what you're telling me now what you'll say if you get called to testify?"

"I guess. I never seen much that night, but I knew he was the one up there. I was asleep when he came down to Murphy's room, but the commotion woke me. If it's my opinion you want, then it's that he killed her, waited for a while to make sure, and then came for Murphy."

I nodded. "Thank you."

The bartender brought her a fresh drink. She had half a million coming, so I left her to pay for it.

The Clarkson brothers sat quietly in their booth muttering to each other. I stopped in front of it.

"My name's Jack Fort," I said. "I got appointed to defend Jesse. Someone pointed you out as friends of his."

The oldest brother nodded up at me. "We know him some, me and Chester. But we've both had our own legal troubles and it wouldn't be smart to call us to help him."

"You're Del then?"

He nodded. "Known to one and all."

They were both big men, larger than me. I figured Del was pushing or past forty, his brother a few years younger. Both of them wore rough wool shirts, jeans, and work boots.

"Were you gentlemen past the house on the night Jesse's aunt died?"

Del Clarkson looked over at his brother. "I ain't sure. How about you, Chet?"

Chet shook his head, watching his brother and not me.

"There are those who say you were," I said.

Del shrugged. "Even if we were, and I'm not saying it's so, we was never inside the house. Jesse never asked us in, not ever. You ask him. He'll tell you."

"All I'm trying to do is establish some times. If you were past the house, I'd like to know what time it was. Jesse's aunt died between nine and ten that night. If you were around about that time, it could help Jesse."

"We'd sure like to help him," Del said heartily. "The thing is we don't want no cop trouble and we hear Jesse's dead meat. So I guess our answer to you is that we been past the house before and maybe we were past that night, but don't remember for sure." He lifted his beer bottle, inspected it, and drank from it.

"That's sure the way of it," Chet said. "You tell Jesse that's all we know, but that we'll be pulling for him and hoping he walks." He slid sideways in the booth and put his feet up, watching me now.

I smiled and nodded. At a trial I'd first establish they were on the scene by other witnesses, then call them, treat them as hostile witnesses and muddy things with them. But in a petition to let to bail they'd be useless.

"Thanks boys," I said. There was no need now to alienate them by giving them a glimpse of my plans. I turned to go.

"Hey now, lawyer man," Del said to my back. "You make sure you tell friend Jess how we're thinking and worrying about him."

"Sure," I said, not turning back.

In the morning, very early, without having received a call from Chicken, I drove to Bloomington, about a two-hour drive.

At a phone booth on the edge of Bloomington I found an address for a Ted Moss listed. It was under the name Theodore C. Moss on West Second.

So much for confidential informants.

I knew the town a little and so I drove in that way and found the house. It was a small shotgun with a one-car port on the side. A nondescript Olds, a couple of years newer than my Plymouth and with better tires and more paint, sat in the carport. I parked up the street and walked back laboriously, my legs having stiffened in the car.

I knocked on the door. A small black boy, maybe four or five years old, with a pinched, thin face came and started to open the door, but then abandoned the job when someone called sharply to him from inside the house.

I waited.

The man who came to the door was blue-black and in his late twenties, athletic-looking, with wise eyes older than his years. He looked me over carefully. He had a hand in a heavy jacket pocket.

"Are you Ted Moss?"

"Yes. And I guess you'd be Jack Fort?"

"Yes. If you'll promise not to shoot me with that pocket gun, I'll dig out some identification."

"You do that," he said. "Real careful."

I showed him a driver's license and a credit card with my name on it.

He relaxed a little. "I guess you're okay or Chicken would never have told you nothin', but I'm supposed to be undercover kind of, at least down there in Scannelsville."

"Your name and address are in the phone book."

"Must have been an old book. I had it taken out this year."

"Did Chicken tell you your drug case had been dismissed?"

He nodded.

"It was dismissed after a murder charge was filed against Jesse DeAlter."

"Chicken said it was the same day. Jesse did sell me some cocaine that night."

"I don't doubt it. He told me what happened." The wind on the porch was starting to pick up and my legs, already stiff, were cramping a little.

"You let me pat you down and then maybe we can go inside," Moss said. "I watched you park and walk up. You were moving funny, like maybe you've got a shotgun down your pants or something."

"Pat away."

He did and I endured it.

When he was satisfied I had no weapons, he said, "Hows come you to move like that?"

"Bad wheels."

"Come on inside where it's warm, bad wheels."

I followed behind him and sat down gratefully in a chair he pointed to. From the hall nearby, a larger boy than the one who'd first come to the door looked me over. Moss smiled fondly at him.

"Go back and watch the television with your brother," Moss said. "I'll take you both on in a bit."

The boy vanished.

The state policeman turned back to me. "So Jesse killed someone on the same day he sold me cocaine?"

"Maybe. It's what sent me here. What time did you make your buy from him?"

"A little before nine that night. The case report would probably show the exact time. Wait and I'll get it." He got up and walked out of the room. I sat in the chair and stretched my legs and liked the warmth.

In a few moments Moss reappeared.

"Eight fifty-nine P.M.," he said. "Our business didn't take long to transact. I went to the big house where he was staying and Jess was watching for me from a window. I bought a packet from him, not much. I tried to pay him in money that had been premarked, but he wouldn't take it. He said he'd collect later, so I didn't push. I let it go. He'd had a drink or three and maybe something else. He's hard to read. But I had lots of things going in your town, Fort. I wasn't about to bust him until they were tied down good."

"Why give him the marked money then?"

"There was a reason. I gave the drugs on to the locals who were watching nearby."

"Did you think it unusual when he wouldn't take the money?"

"Peculiar is all." He thought for a moment. "Sometimes guys like Jess will wait to trade when they got a need."

"Then he wasn't a professional dealer?"

"I'd guess no, but I don't really know for certain." He looked me over. My legs were hurting some.

"Want hot coffee? I got a pot on the stove. I got to take the one boy to school and the other to the sitters, but there's time for some coffee."

"Please. Black."

He nodded approval and went to the kitchen. I could hear him rattling around out there. In a few moments he returned with cups of coffee. I took the one he offered and drank some down. It was hot and good. My legs seemed to be loosening in the heat.

"Tell me how Jesse acted in more detail if you can. Was he nervous?"

"No. And he wasn't out of it. He'd had some drinks and maybe something else, pot or cocaine. I'd been around town for a while and he knew me, but we weren't friends. Come to think on it, he had no real friends. He usually acted to me like someone who didn't give a damn. The only time I ever saw anything out of him was when he'd talk about Vietnam. He lost a brother there."

"Half brother," I corrected.

"Okay. I think it bothered him that he'd hid out in Canada while his half brother died in Vietnam."

"Based on what you saw that night, did you have any idea he was a man planning a murder?"

"That's a crazy question. I don't know who can kill or when they will kill. I've dealt with killers as young as fifteen and as old as eighty. I've had them who killed because they wanted money or drugs or a tank of gas. I've had lots who killed for hate and a few who killed for love."

"All right, I'll buy that. But to me it's what makes you an expert. Sometime after you were past, and not very long after, Jesse is supposed to have put a pillow over his sick, old aunt's face and suffocated her. Maybe he did this after feeding her drugs and some booze."

"I have no opinion," he said. "I will say, if he was planning on running, he might have wanted every dime he could lay together. He'd have collected from me. Or maybe," he said, shaking his head, "if he figured on coming into money, he'd not want mine."

"How many times had you been around him prior to the night you made the buy?"

"Lots of times." He scratched his head. "He wasn't that much into drugs. I watched him some because he was different than my usuals. He'd do a little and then he'd get terrified and cold-turkey and break the habit. You see some like that—ones who want to test or punish themselves. I kept after him to get me a real buy, but he never did. He ain't the best case I ever put together, but the locals were satisfied with it at first."

"He wrote a book once," I said, remembering what Karen and Abe had said about it.

"Did he now. He seemed bright at times. I got into that county working undercover when the locals asked for someone to come in. I met a few medium dealers. Jesse was small-time." He looked up at me. "You never catch the big timers. You start sniffing close and people who know things run or die."

"Would Jesse know anyone up the ladder?"

"Maybe. He was someone they could find usable. He came from a good family and had been to college. But he might also be a problem because he had no job and he and his ex-wife were all the time fighting."

"Did you ever meet his ex-wife?" I asked, worried about what his answer might be.

"No. I saw her once or twice. Good-looking woman."

A sound came from one of the far rooms. He cocked his head and looked at his watch. "Schooltime, Fort. My wife leaves early for her job and I'm the father bear."

"Yes." I handed him a subpoena. "This is for tomorrow, but I doubt we'll want you. How about we call the Bloomington post if we do and if you don't get our call, then don't come?"

He frowned at the subpoena, which I'd prepared from blanks supplied by the county clerk, but brightened at my words.

"That's fair. Give me about a two-hour lead."

I drove back to Scannelsville. There was time to stop
past the jail and carefully discuss with a curious (and for
once semi-humble) Jesse what would happen that afternoon.

I lunched on a Big Mac. I then went to the office and
collected Abe. Together we walked to the courthouse. We
were fifteen minutes early.

"What's your final strategy to be?" Abe asked as we
stood by our counsel table. He was nervous and watching
him affected me. Part of my nervousness was from doubts
about it being good for him to be here in the shabby, cold
courtroom that smelled of mildew, dampness, and old
defeats. I thought it might be worse for him if he wasn't
here, for in the courtroom he had purpose, but I remembered Doc Jacobsen's words . . .

Everyone is terminal.

Nearby, at the state's counsel table, Al came with his
two deputies and two police officers. Now and then he'd
look our way sourly. One time his voice got loud enough
for us to hear him.

"Waste of valuable time," he said loudly, glaring at me.

I nodded. "That's what we thought about your case also.
It isn't too late for you to dismiss the indictment and save
yourself embarrassment."

He shook his head in fury. It was one of his better
moves.

Petitions to let to bail are oddball proceedings in Indiana. Some years before I'd come to Scannelsville, the Indiana General Assembly (in its dubious but collective wis-
dom) had adopted a new criminal code and repealed
many old statutes. The right to be let to bail had existed
under the old law and it continued afterward, being nor-

mally used as a discovery tool for those accused of non-bailable offenses, a sort of up-front view of what evidence the state had and desired to present. But the hearing could be more than that. Bail could be granted. It rarely was, but I'd heard of it happening.

The procedure followed was that the defendant presented evidence first and then the state could call witnesses.

I'd call Jesse. He'd take all afternoon. Then I'd decide whether or not to call the state trooper and some of the other witnesses who'd testified before the grand jury. Maybe, if I got lucky, I could just go with Jesse plus a stipulated introduction of the grand jury tapes.

Plus, if necessary, my inside man at the jail, Silent Bill. I'd winked at him earlier when I'd gone in to see Jesse. All I'd gotten in return was a look which tried to place me. When Bill was undercover, I guessed he was determined about it.

The only direct, damaging evidence I'd heard about Jesse in the tapes was about the initial on the sheet and the evidence of Annie Tinker.

My bet was there'd be more.

If the evidence wasn't clear and convincing, the judge could grant bail.

Jesse had no money, no expectations. Bail would be impossible for him to make. Still, if it was set, there was always a chance.

Two deputies brought Jesse over from jail and we began.

Seven or eight media people had made it to the hearing plus maybe a dozen locals. Spectators sat here and there in the large courtroom, tiny islands surrounded by the deep waters of empty seats. Most of the watchers seemed already bored.

I thought the trial itself would draw well because people like, these days, to wander in and out of murder trial courtrooms about as much as they like dirty movies. But preliminaries don't draw flies.

Jesse was sworn. He nodded up at the judge and I wondered how well they knew each other. Too late now.

I went through identifying questions, name, address, education, and even, coldly, his current marital status. I found myself hard at work for now, with no interest in Karen other than as a statistic in Jesse's life. I was bought and paid for, a hundred-dollar (plus county pay) advocate.

Al Windham watched me warily from his counsel table, ready to pounce. His two deputies made notes and passed them to him as I progressed. The deputies were young, dewy, and dressed in their best three-piece suits. One of them had curly hair, the other was going bald. I'd heard younger lawyers in the local bar call them "Curly" and "Moe," professing not to know their real names. Imports, brought in by Al.

I asked Jesse, "You've been indicted for the killing of Ruth DeAlter. You know you have no obligation to testify and can't be required to, but you want to testify—is that it?"

"Yes. I want to testify both here and in the trial if a trial ever becomes necessary."

"You're the defendant and have been in jail for about a week now, held without bond?"

"Yes sir."

"Can you tell the court anything about your aunt's demise?"

Jesse sat up alertly in the witness chair. For a man in

chains who'd been in jail for about a week he looked pretty decent. "I found her sometime shortly before eleven o'clock. I've heard she'd been dead for a while before I did find her and maybe had died between nine and ten."

"What makes you think she'd been dead for a time before you found her?"

"I touched her skin. It was cool. I then went downstairs and found James, her handyman, and we called the emergency squad."

"Who was it who called the police?"

"I'm not sure who made that call. It wasn't me. I rode with my aunt in the emergency ambulance to the hospital. I stayed there and was arrested at the hospital after some calls between the police and the prosecutor's office."

"Did the police ask you any questions at the hospital?"

"Lots of questions."

"And did you answer those questions?"

"Of course."

"When you answered these early questions for the police, were you intoxicated in any way?"

"No. I'd had a couple of drinks very early and the drinks made me sleepy. So I slept. I was okay when I woke up."

"After a time, did someone read you what are called your Miranda rights?"

"Later. Not at first."

"Tell me about your room and where it is in relation to your aunt's room?"

"It adjoins it."

"And the house is hers? You've no legal interest in it?"

"It's her house. She wanted me in that room. She asked

me to move there. I stayed there every time I was in her house."

"What prompted you to go into her room that night at eleven o'clock or so?"

"I checked on her almost every night. Sometimes it would be later than that night, sometimes earlier. She had a small bell she rang, but sometimes I'd knock and then go in, whether I heard it or not. I woke up and I went to her room." He looked up at the judge. "I went in to see if she needed anything."

"Did you wake up for any particular reason—noise, a call—like that?"

"I don't remember anything in particular—just waking up as I've done on countless other nights and going into her room to check her."

"Describe her appearance when you first saw her after entering her room."

"Cool, dark, waxen, and not visibly breathing. Her pillow was off the bed on the floor. She was face down, but her face was turned out so I could see her features. Her eyes were open. Her blankets were pulled out at the bottom of her bed."

"Did you kill her, Jesse?"

"Certainly not. She was an old woman. Both of us knew she had very little time left. Even if I'd hated her, which I didn't, why would I kill her?"

I ignored his question. "On that night did you give her any pills, drugs, or whiskey?"

He hesitated and then nodded. "She wanted a shot glass of whiskey early on, like maybe eight o'clock. I gave it to her. And she was physically able to get more if she wanted it. And she kept a boatload of pills close that she used when she wanted to use them."

"Did you touch her when you entered her bedroom that last time?"

"Her face with a finger."

"Did you know she wasn't supposed to have any alcoholic beverages."

"Of course," he said. "So did she, but she'd ask for it. And, in moderation, I'd supply it. Annie Tinker would buy it for her." Jesse smiled tolerantly. "Along with a touch for herself. Irish whiskey for Annie, Scotch for my aunt."

"There was some testimony before the grand jury that you and your aunt fought a lot. Did you do that?"

"Yes. We were a lot alike. We argued and name-called, mostly in card games." He smiled his appealing smile. "She cheated at cards. And I'm far from a perfect man. She could be very scathing when she dug into my personal habits, very hurtful."

I moved on. I got him to tell the story of his relationship with his aunt from early in his life until the day of her death. Now and then I could stand away and watch Judge Westley and attempt to read his reaction. He seemed interested.

At a quarter after four I felt I was done. I turned to Abe. He nodded at me, thinking it was enough also. I looked up at the clock and smiled at Al Windham, waiting in anticipation.

"You may cross-examine," I said.

The judge looked up at the clock also. He frowned. "Will you be long, Mr. Prosecutor?"

"I'd doubt it, your honor."

"We'll go on for a bit then."

Al went after Jesse like a fisherman after a game fish. "You were her heir?" he asked.

Jesse smiled. "You know I wasn't. You were her lawyer

and someone in your firm prepared her most recent will. She left me only a pittance."

"And you knew that and became angry about it. Didn't you kill her to punish her?"

"No."

"Didn't she call you into her room and read you her latest will that night?"

It was an area where Jesse and I had conferred. "No. She didn't read it to me and I didn't read it myself. My lawyer, after the fact, told me I could be recompensed for the care I gave her. I also understand she left a great deal of her money to worthy causes." He smiled amiably.

"You've filed a claim for most of her estate," Al said. "Isn't that correct?"

"I only want to be paid what I'm entitled to. That's something for you and my lawyer to work out."

"Didn't you go into her room and smother her?"

"No."

"Then you must know who did. You were only a few feet away. Didn't you tell the police that you didn't see or hear anything?"

"I didn't."

"And your aunt died a few feet away?"

"A few feet, a wall, and a closed door away," Jesse said.

Al turned and smiled at me, his back to Jesse. "Who initialed her sheet with your initial as she was dying?"

"I don't know. I never saw any initial that night. Just some kind of ink mark and a pen."

"It's unfortunate for you the police did," Al said.

I thought about objecting, but sat still. Abe nodded his approval.

"Sometimes I sleep very soundly, particularly after a few drinks. Assuming someone else came into the house and killed my aunt, that habit may have saved my life. Or maybe I wasn't even inside the house when she was killed. I was in and out of my room some that night. In fact that's how I originally wound up in jail."

Next to me I saw Abe holding both of his hands below the counsel table, silently applauding.

"Didn't you constantly encourage her to take drugs and give her booze and pills?"

"No. She fed them to herself and decided whether to take them of her own volition," Jesse answered patiently. "She hurt and she said that sometimes, at night, a touch of alcohol helped. It was also hard for her to fall asleep and so she'd take pills for that and other things. She'd ring and one of us in the house would give her what she wanted."

"What about this pillow on the floor? Was your aunt right- or left-handed?"

"Right."

"Explain to the judge why the pillow was off on the left side of her bed?"

"Not having been present when she or someone else placed or threw the pillow where it was found, I can't even hazard a guess," Jesse said.

"Where was the pillow in relation to the door between your room and your aunt's?" Al asked, as if it was damning evidence.

"My recollection was that the pillow was quite close to the door."

"Did you drop it there in a panic after you smothered your aunt?" Al asked darkly.

Jesse chuckled. "No. I hope I seem smarter than that to most people, even if not to you."

Windham considered Jesse. "I ask questions. You answer them. No arguments. No comments. Just answers."

"Ask me questions then," Jesse said tartly. "Don't make ridiculous comments and then ask me to respond to them."

The prosecutor looked up at the judge, his attitude one of long suffering. "Your honor . . ."

"Continue, Mr. Windham," Judge Westley said primly.

I looked down at the counsel table and stifled a smile. Abe shuffled papers in front of him and failed to hide his own grin.

"Are you addicted to any drugs, Mr. DeAlter?"

"No. I've experimented with drugs, but I'm not an addict."

"How about alcohol?"

"Ah, that's a different matter. Sometimes I've drunk a dab too much," Jesse answered. "Not recently, of course."

"You mean because you're in jail?"

"Yes," Jesse said.

"How well do you get on with the other prisoners over in the local jail?" Al asked innocently.

"What do you mean?"

"Well, you're born to the purple, a sort of local aristocrat, with an education. How did that affect your relationship with other prisoners in the jail?"

"It didn't. I go my way and they go their way." Jesse smiled. "Yesterday the sheriff put some guy in a cell close to me who can't hear or talk. We get on very well."

I found the counsel tabletop again. I'd seen Silent Bill that morning, but I'd not known that Jesse had noticed him.

"Would you know a prisoner in the jail named Carson Stonewaite? I believe he may be nicknamed 'Skinny.'"

"I know which one he is. Good old 'Skin.' Kind of a high-grade burglar."

Beside me Abe furiously scribbled something on a yellow pad and pushed at me. Al Windham watched us and waited for a minute.

I read Abe's message: "You can buy Skinny for a dollar or a day off his sentence."

Al went on casually: "Did you ever say to Mr. Stonewaite that you killed your aunt in the hopes of getting her money?"

"Of course not. I didn't say it or do it."

"Sure?"

"Of course I'm sure."

"Is Mr. Stonewaite an enemy of yours?"

"Not that I know of," Jesse said.

Al smiled. He looked up at the clock. "I'd like to stop for now and then begin again tomorrow."

Judge Westley nodded agreeably. He looked over at Abe and then at me. "Okay, gentlemen?"

"Yes," I said.

"Two o'clock tomorrow then," Judge Westley said.

I left Abe's company and followed Jesse back to jail. When we were at his cell and the deputy had gone, I got very close to the bars and asked, "Did you say anything at all to this Skinny Stonewaite?"

Jesse nodded. "They'd left me pretty much alone. Last night they moved him back closer to me, him and that dummy over there." He nodded over at Silent Bill, who studiously ignored me. "Skinny asked me some stuff about Canada. He said he'd heard I'd been there. He never asked me a single question about my aunt. Not a one."

"All right, but from now on in, like I instructed you before, say nothing at all."

"How about my wife? How about asking you what happened to you in Vietnam?" He leaned against the cell wall, eyes mocking.

"Get funny and you may spend a long, long time regretting it."

"Come on, Fort. You're not going to get me out. My aunt's dead and it looked to me, when I first saw her, like someone had killed her. I almost ran and I guess I should have. I'm the best and easiest thing they've got for a suspect. So don't fool with my hopes. I've screwed up my life real well without you and I guess I can now screw it up more in prison." He grinned amiably. "First thing I ever got accused of where I didn't do the dirty deed or worse."

"Stick with me a while longer. Do what I tell you to do."

He sighed. "I guess maybe I should do that until, inevitably, I find out your feet are made out of poor, old Indiana clay."

We began watching from Mrs. Headley's house before six.

It was not quite dusk and there was still a crowd of people in the yard of the DeAlter place left over from the auction of the afternoon. Some workmen were gathering up odds and ends out of the yard and carrying them back into the mansion.

Mrs. Headley watched with us out of her second-floor windows. She sniffed with satisfaction, perhaps for my benefit.

"No one bought the house. The appraisal was too high. I could have told them that up front. And trying to wheedle someone into buying that monster took lots of the auctioneer's time. They had to sell the last bunch of boxed stuff as a lot and there were still some minor things around unsold." She smiled at Karen, liking her, perhaps unsure why Karen had brought me along. "I bought a rose vase. I paid too much, but it's a nice piece. One of the few non-gaudy things she had. For all her money, the woman had no taste at all. Michael had all the taste in that family. He knew paintings and antiques and stamps and coins and lots of things."

"How large was the crowd?" Karen asked.

"Huge. They milled around all over the place and blocked traffic. But there weren't very many serious buyers. Mostly curious people wanting to see what a murdered woman had."

Karen moved closer to the window where Mrs. Headley watched and the two women stared out together. Someone turned on the outer lights of the DeAlter house.

I had my own window. I watched out of the old, flawed pane. Some cars and trucks remained parked in front of the house. As time passed and it grew darker, the remains of the crowd diminished. My window distorted my view, but I could see well enough.

I saw James Murphy leave the house. He was carrying two large suitcases and he put them in the trunk of the elderly four-door Cadillac I'd seen before.

"That's old Murphy who worked for Ruth," Mrs. Headley said, not knowing I'd met him. "He bought her old car today and paid almost four thousand dollars for it. There were two used car dealers bidding against him, but he outbid them. I guess it's a good car even if it is out of style. He'd know better than anyone, having taken care of it. I've heard some say that, when they were younger, he and Ruth were lovers, but I never saw anything to indicate it."

"You think it was just gossip?" I asked, interested.

She shrugged, not knowing.

Murphy put his bags in the back seat of the car and reentered the house. The outer lights of the house were turned off. In a while Murphy reappeared at the front door carrying a large box.

"Moving on," Mrs. Headley said knowingly.

"How about the other one? Annie Tinker?"

"She left about four. Some men came by and picked her up, bags, boxes, and all." She sniffed again. "In my opinion she'd already been drinking. And last night it was after one when she got home. Those thieving Clarkson brothers brought her in an old car."

"Have you seen them with her before?" I asked.

"A few times," Mrs. Headley said.

We waited some more. It got dark outside and the only light came from a street lamp in the alley on the far side of the house. Without lights the old house looked cold and forbidding.

Someone stood on the side street and watched the house for a time, but then moved on.

Mrs. Headley finally gave up and went to bed after making us a pot of coffee. We thanked her for the coffee and kept watching, sitting in chairs by the window. It was dark out, but from here we could see and not be seen.

I could sense Mrs. Headley in her bed a few doors away, listening.

"She's very curious about you," Karen whispered.

"She's very curious about everything."

"She wonders out loud about how and why you're living here in Scannelsville. She makes guesses about what's wrong with you." She smiled. "I thought she'd never give up helping us watch. All this is a very big thing in her life."

"My bet is we won't be long with her. If someone's out

there waiting and watching, he, she, or they will get impatient before long."

"Couldn't it have been anyone watching for any reason, before or after Ruth died?"

"Yes."

She thought on that for a moment.

"There's a soft chair in the corner. You could take a nap there for a while. I'll watch and then wake you up later."

I thought about doing that. I'd been up before dawn and on the road. I'd spent the afternoon in the courtroom where a minute can be an hour, but I wasn't tired—at least not yet.

"Not sleepy," I said. "You sleep."

"I'll be wide awake for a time yet. Then sometime after midnight I'll turn into a disaster area. But it won't matter because tomorrow's my day off."

I checked her over. She had on no-nonsense jeans, not the skintight, but the soft, loose ones. She wore a bulky sweater. I thought she might have dressed both for comfort and also so as not to affect me. The latter hadn't worked.

"I doubt your ability to turn into a disaster area even if you tried hard."

"A compliment," she said, eyes widening. "Thank you, kind sir."

"I'm sure it's not your first."

She nodded complacently. "Most these days come from doctors who are happily or unhappily married and looking for that special someone to share the moments of stolen good times. They're better than those from Jesse's pals who used to get far enough off the world so they'd forget who I was." She looked at me in the dim light that entered the window. "Did you ever do any drugs, Jack?"

"In high school I got dared and I took a drag off a joint. It didn't do much for me except make me a little nauseated. I was into athletics then, baseball and basketball. I was good enough at baseball to get asked to some tryouts. I thought maybe I'd play in the service but they had other ideas. In the air I needed to be as good as I could be. I didn't drink then, not even beer. I took no drugs I wasn't ordered to take by a doctor."

"Did you like the Navy?"

"I liked flying. I liked the carrier I was on and the people I flew with. What I saw of Vietnam I saw from the air. Green and brown, hills and valleys, pretty when I'd first see it, ugly sometimes when I left it."

She moved in her chair so as to face me more.

"I liked nursing on the hospital ship. It was clean and correct and I felt, for the first time in my life, like I was doing something important."

"But you left."

She looked away from me and out into the street. "For a time I didn't care that my doctor was married and then I did. So I left." She turned back to me. "Forget that. Tell me more about where you come from. About Jack."

"My family's gone. I was an only child, my father an only child, and my mother had one brother who got killed in Korea. My folks died when I was in a stateside hospital —a commercial plane crash. There are some distant cousins scattered here and there, but I'd not recognize any of them if I saw them."

"What made you come to Scannelsville?"

I kept my eyes away from hers, fearful that she'd read them. "I wonder myself at times." I watched the yard across the street.

Nothing.

"I was in a big firm in Chicago. I did trial work, representing insurance companies. I spent my days and sometimes my nights picking holes in plaintiff's stories, trying for defendants' verdicts or a favorable settlement. I woke up one day and discovered I didn't want to do it any longer. I didn't mind taking on the cheats, but I couldn't stomach hurting people who'd already been losers. So I quit and somehow wandered down here."

"And you say you're not married?"

"I promise," I said, smiling. "I've never been married."

Her eyes seemed troubled. "Some people who get injured as badly as you were injured hide inside themselves. They can't or won't form or hold on to relationships because that closeness would let someone else discover the hurt. Are you single because of your legs, Jack?"

"I don't know. I'd hope not. There was law school first off and it was hard and time-consuming for me. Then there was the Chicago firm. It was worse, but there have been some girls."

She smiled, maybe liking my answer. "Not very many girls, I'll bet. Not as many as there ought to have been. But you look good." She nodded her head at my unbelieving smile. "You do look good. Jesse is so handsome he's pretty. You just look good, clean, and trim and your eyes are kind."

"That's enough of both Jesse and me for now," I said. "To keep me awake, why not tell me more about you?"

She shrugged. "I got some scholarships and I thought I had to be a nurse and maybe, sometime, a doctor. I left Scannelsville and I thought I'd never return, but I did of course. Most of the men in my family, back the years, worked in the mines, some in the DeAlter mines. Some of them died, some of them lived. I'm part Irish, part English, some German, and way back the line, American Indian. A little bit of everything. I came back here because I was homesick for my own people. Suddenly there was Jesse and he was so beautiful. So I took jobs in nursing homes, doctors' offices, and now at the hospital to support him and the books he was going to write. No children and none expected." She looked out into the night and changed the subject. "Do you really believe someone will come to Ruth's house?"

"Maybe. And tonight would be a good time."

"Why?"

"Because it's the first night it's been empty." I thought some on it. "If not tonight, then it'll be soon if someone is really out there waiting. We'll watch for a few nights."

The watcher came early in the morning. I was surprised. It had been a long chance.

Peering out the window was sleep-inducing after we ran short of conversation, so we split the night into segments, spelling each other every two hours in the dark room.

Only the single street lamp gave illumination, but after watching for a time, it was enough. The light was a shadow-caster, leaving dark spots where the house blocked its way.

"What happens if we actually see something?" Karen asked.

I found I'd not thought that far. "I think I'll have you call the police and the sheriff and I'll go out and try to get close enough to see the person interested in Ruth's house."

"That might be dangerous."

"I'll be very quiet. I just need to see who it is, not capture them."

She shook her head. "We should both stay right here and call the authorities."

"No. Police coming could very well scare whoever comes off and away forever."

"You might get hurt," she said darkly.

"I'll be careful and not take any chances."

She glanced down at my legs, perhaps remembering that I'd taken chances before and lost.

We watched.

The intruder came late, almost three in the morning. I sensed someone out there before I saw them. Karen slept silently in her chair. I touched her chair and she came awake.

"Out there," I said.

"Where?"

"See where the fountain's edge is? Something went past it a moment ago. Whoever it is is in the shadows now."

She shook her head to clear it.

"I'm going over there. You wait a few moments until I'm across the street and into the yard. Then you call both the police and sheriff."

She nodded. Her eyes met mine and I could read fear in them.

"Remember," I said from the room door. "You wait until I'm in the yard."

I went down the steps. I let myself out into the yard and went silently through the front gate. Tiny drops of freezing rain made the street slick and the wind had come up, but I made it across. I went through the archway into the DeAlter yard. I raised a hand so that Karen would see me. Then I moved carefully along the side of the house in darkness. I felt more than saw a side door I'd not known was there. It was closed and would not yield to my touch.

I moved on.

There was no moon. Out of the light from the street-light beyond the house it was completely dark. But, in the darkness, my eyes adjusted a little.

In the backyard there was light and I found it. The back door was also tight when I touched it. Fifteen feet past the back door were the double doors down into the cellar. One of the doors had been raised.

Steps led down. I followed them.

From inside the basement I could hear sounds. Some-one was tapping in the deeper darkness. The sound seemed to come from the top of the steps to the first floor. I saw a ray of light from a flashlight. I moved that way and then stood and listened some more. I heard more sounds. This time it was not tapping. Someone was using a tool to rip at the wood of the door above.

I stepped forward and my foot came down wrong and I stumbled. All sound above me stopped. I moved toward the source. I heard sounds again, closer, moving my way. Something or someone passed me quickly and I threw up my hands and touched cloth. A metal thing sang past my eyes whipping up the wind. I ducked and felt a tiny sting-ing on my forehead above my eyes. I tried to grapple in the darkness. The gloved hands that pushed me away seemed smaller than my own. My own hands, strong from the days when my legs wouldn't work, were stronger. I caught at the intruder and hung on. Something cold slashed past me again, but this time I got a hand and held it. A piece of metal, I thought it to be a knife, clattered against the basement floor.

I got in a good punch and felt the body I grappled with go limp.

I made sure that both hands of my assailant were emptied and then did a body search. There was a flashlight in a jacket and I dropped that on the floor.

Whoever it was seemed small now. I pulled the body to the steps and up them.

In the backyard in the light, the rain came down hard and cold.

My assailant wore a mask. I stripped it away. The face under the mask was not unknown.

It was Mildred Marsh, the lady who'd claimed an interest in the history of Scannelsville. I put a finger on the pulse in her neck. It beat strongly.

I heard Karen calling my name.

"Back here."

I saw her come into the backyard.

Mildred Marsh stirred. "Help me with her," I said to Karen.

"Both lines were busy," she said. "I finally called the operator." She touched my head. "You're bleeding."

I touched my forehead. It was wet and, when I looked at my fingers, they were black in the light.

Mildred Marsh's eyes opened.

"Lay very still or I'll hit you again," I said.

Her hands sought something and then gave up.

"It's probably on the floor in the DeAlter basement," I said. "Who the hell are you really?"

"Mildred Marsh," she said. "I was just looking around."

"No. More than that."

She watched me and hated me.

Sheriff Goldie came. He was dressed sloppily and he looked sleepy.

"What are you into now, Fort?" he asked suspiciously. He eyed the woman on the ground between Karen and me.

I explained. I found a handkerchief in my pocket and wiped at the cut on my forehead.

Another police car, lights and siren on, came.

Mildred Marsh sat up. She eyed the cast coolly and waited.

"I was just looking around," she said finally.

Goldie got out a card and read her Miranda rights to her.

"Watch her," he told the city officers.

I showed him the raised basement door. He took a flashlight and we went down and into the basement.

Where I'd collided with Mildred Marsh, there was a flashlight, a wrecking bar and a sharp knife. The door at the top of the steps to the upper floors had pry marks on it.

"She was working on something before she went up the steps. Tapping the walls maybe. It sounded that way."

In the light of the flashlight we inspected the walls and found a light switch. Goldie flipped it on.

The walls were dusty, but there were marks on them in the dust. There were places where the stone had been chipped.

"Who is she?" Goldie asked me.

"I'm not sure. She came to Abe and wanted information on the town. He's been helping her."

"I'll charge her with burglary and maybe attempted murder," Goldie said. "Will you sign an information?"

"Yes."

Goldie thought ponderously for a moment. "Could she be a he? I hear you been asking questions about Jesse's brother Peter. Could that be Peter?"

I shook my head. The person I'd caught and searched was a woman.

Goldie took her to jail.

Karen took me back to Mrs. Headley's place and used tape borrowed there and cut in shapes like butterflies to put my head back together.

She gave me a light kiss after that, her eyes excited. I wondered if the excitement this new development had brought might be mostly for Jesse, but I didn't ask.

I dreamed of the encounter while I slept out the rest of the night. In the dreams sometimes I won, but most times I lost. But my antagonist was a man, and not Mildred Marsh.

I called Abe first thing in the morning and told him what had happened. He seemed upset.

"I'll check out the old lady who was with her, Mrs. Flint. You go ahead with your hearing this afternoon if the prosecutor doesn't dismiss."

"You told me those two women evidenced no interest in the DeAlters."

His voice was puzzled. "They didn't. I'll check with the sheriff also and see if he's gotten anything out of her." He paused. "You sound tired. Go back to sleep for a while."

I did and slept until noon.

I went past the office at one-thirty in the afternoon, but Abe was out.

I walked on to the jail and went in to see Jesse. As I walked past Silent Bill's cell, he gave me a tiny nod and a smile.

"Maybe it does have to do with my half brother," Jesse said. "I heard about it, or some of it, when they brought her in last night. Was she really in the basement?"

"She was. And she really cut me with a knife."

"And she was trying to get into the house?"

"Yes. She'd also hacked at the walls with the pry bar. Does that give you any ideas?"

"No. Not really. There were people who did all kinds of things looking for my father's money when he died, but no one ever found a thing."

"Where did they look?"

"About every place imaginable?"

"In the house?"

"Sure. And the basement also." He thought for a moment. "My father never let us play down there and Ruth kept the rule after he died."

I waited while he thought.

"Peter's dead. He has to be dead," Jesse said strongly, shaking his head. "The bastard can't be alive. But maybe . . ."

"Tell me what you're thinking."

"There was this big family blowup when he took off. My father was already somewhat lost in the head. Peter stole something when he left that was our father's."

"What exactly did he take?"

"Nothing stuff really. A pen and ink drawing of the house as it was before and after my father enlarged it. Then, some money. Some other stuff, mine diagrams, some of his mother's things."

"Did Peter hate your father?"

"Peter? Oh yes. He hated all, everyone. He'd get up in the morning and begin to figure how to burn out the world. By noon he'd figure a way to begin. By nightfall he'd be halfway home to getting the job done."

"When I was checking, I heard that both of you were into that kind of conduct."

Jesse smiled without apology. "I suppose we were, but not in concert. We were alike in many extra ways for persons who may or may not have been blood relations, according to who told it. He was just better at dealing with things than me. I was bored. He was active."

"Did he look like you?"

"Some."

"Was it your father or your aunt who ran him off?"

"My father was sick then. He knew things, but he'd forget them two minutes after he knew them. He lived in a world where old people go when they begin to leave this one. Aunt Ruth found out about the missing money. She made Peter leave. The other stuff that was missing wasn't discovered until Peter was gone."

"Could he still be alive?" I asked him and myself.

He shrugged. "Maybe you'd know more about that kind of possibility than I would. Could a soldier fake his own death in Vietnam?"

"What outfit was he in?"

"He was some kind of Green Beret I think."

I remembered the carrier I'd flown from. "I couldn't have done it, but maybe someone on land could have. It's doubtful. Abe wired Washington. We'll find out what they say, for whatever that means."

We fell silent, both of us thinking. I caught one more glimpse of Silent Bill when the sheriff came for Jesse. When I passed his cell, he winked broadly.

Al Windham was already in the courtroom when we entered. Abe had not yet appeared.

Al signaled he wanted a conference. Judge Westley smiled his approval. I followed Al to the back of the courtroom. Outside the wind whipped flakes of snow against the long windows.

"The sheriff says you and he caught someone in the DeAlter place last night. I tried to talk to the lady this morning, but got nothing from her."

I waited.

"Maybe we could hold this up for a few days and let me look over this new situation?"

"And could we let my man out of jail while that's going on?"

"Of course not. He's been indicted for murder."

"Let's move on then," I said. "You do what you think is right about what took place last night and we'll go on with the petition to let to bail."

"You're a real ass," he said, quickly furious, as was his way. "Here I'm offering to take another look and you insist on going on with this senseless hearing. There's sufficient evidence to hold Jesse, no matter what happened last night. To shorten things, if you'll agree, after I finish with Jesse I'm going to ask the judge to listen to the grand jury tapes. If you don't want it that way, I'll call the witnesses who testified, one by one. Plus I've one witness who'll tie things up who didn't appear before the grand jury."

"I'll bet he's a dilly," I said.

"My added witness? You're right about that. You should have told your client to keep shut in jail. He's dug his own grave with his mouth. A smart butt."

"I did warn him," I said, acting unsure.

"You didn't warn him strongly enough," Al said.

I looked away and then back and presented him with my patented worried look.

"I've already listened to the tapes and so, to save time, if you want, I might agree to the court listening to them instead of the individual witnesses."

He examined me for flaws and I gave him my best sincere look in return.

"Maybe we can wrap this up today then," he said, somewhat mollified.

"Could be."

"I apologize for losing my temper the other day in the hall." He looked somberly out at the snow which was sticking some and coming down harder. "I've had a bad temper ever since I was into athletics. At times it helped then, but it's a problem now." He gave me his best "Elect Al" pose. "Please accept my apology and I'll try hard to make certain it doesn't happen again."

"Of course," I said. I watched him and wondered how much muscle there was behind his growing paunch. If there was another time, I'd try to be ready. My feeling was that even as he apologized, he planned ahead. Bully of the block.

I went to our counsel table and wondered where Abe was.

Al eventually finished with Jesse without shaking his story, but he asked enough questions to get the media people their headlines. I let him alone, allowing him to ask away, not objecting to the way he did it.

When he was done, Jesse stepped down and walked back and sat by me, rattling his chains. I gave him a tiny approving pat on the arm and got in return a look of anger.

"He was all over me," Jesse whispered. "How come you didn't object?"

"I didn't need to. I spent part of my time watching the

judge. He was about as irritated as you seem to be. Accusations and loud words mean nothing without proof."

Jesse leaned back in his chair. After a time he nodded. "Okay I guess. But I sure felt like I could have used some help."

Al motioned me to the bench.

Westley leaned toward us politely.

"You will agree to stipulating in the grand jury tapes as evidence?" Al asked.

I frowned and acted as if I was reconsidering it.

"I suppose," I finally said. "It'd save time."

Al nodded quickly. "All I have in addition is one more witness. I've sent the sheriff over to get him."

I went back to the counsel table. Jesse raised his eyebrows.

"We're just about to hear how you confessed to one Carson 'Skinny' Stonewaite."

"Maybe it's about time for you to get tough and do some objecting," Jesse said coldly.

"On the contrary. I'm looking forward eagerly to his testimony."

The sheriff brought the thin man I'd seen before in the jail into the courtroom. He was dressed in old wool pants and a faded plaid shirt, but the clothes were clean and he was clean. He appeared to be fiftyish and he had a habit of blinking his eyes too often, as if he was either nervous or had eye trouble.

The judge swore him in and he took the stand, stated his name, and cheerfully admitted he was now and had been a resident of the Cannell County jail for the past two months for burglarizing a convenience store. Al led him back through other thefts and burglaries, a lengthy list.

"Do you know Jesse DeAlter?" Al asked, pointing at Jesse.

"Sure. Him and me's old pals. He's in jail for killing his aunt." He nodded at me, a friendly man. "That's him and his lawyer there—I've seen the lawyer in coaching him."

"Coaching him?" Al asked.

"Yeah. Telling him what to say and what not to say. You know. Like lawyers do."

Al moved on. "Did Jesse ever tell you anything about his aunt's death?"

"Just last night he started to talk about it some. He told me he needed money and she had it and he thought he was going to get it. So he said he slipped into her bedroom and put a pillow over her face."

"And when was it he told you that?"

"Last night in the jail. I knew you'd be interested and so I had a deputy call you and I told you about it."

"Did you tell me over in the jail?"

"Yes sir, but not in the cell area. You took me out to an office to talk. Then we talked some more in the cell area this morning with Jesse sleeping in the next cell." He shook his head, perplexed by the perfidies of man. "You and me both wondered how someone can sleep as good as Jesse after having done what he done to an old lady."

Jesse nudged me. I frowned him into inaction.

"And have you been promised any leniency or special treatment for testifying here today?"

"No sir."

"Your witness," Al said.

"Thank you," I said. I got to my feet and went near the witness stand. I smiled at Skinny and inspected him. He waited and smiled back. He'd been in a lot of courtrooms.

"You say the prosecutor promised you nothing for testifying here today?"

"Not a thing. No sir, not a single thing."

I turned away and looked out into the courtroom. Out there half a dozen journalists scribbled.

"Positive?"

"Yes, I am," he said virtuously. "I hope he'll treat me good 'cause I've had a lot of trouble in my life, but this trip I've found Jesus and maybe with his help I can turn myself around."

Up close I could tell he was older than I'd at first thought him to be, maybe closer to sixty than fifty, an old thief and burglar who'd seen the jailhouse elephant a dozen-dozen times.

"How many times would you estimate you've been in jail, Mr. Stonewaite?"

Al bobbed up. "Objection. Mr. Fort knows it can't be done this way."

"Sustained," Westley said.

I turned to Al. "You want to agree to letting the court see a printout?"

He inclined his head. "If it'll help get this hearing over, then I'll agree."

I returned to the witness. "Was there anyone else around when you and Jesse were talking or when you and the prosecutor spoke together in the jail while Mr. DeAlter slept?"

Stonewaite shook his head. "No one but me and them guys. The dummy-drunk was across the way in a cell, but all he ever does inside is watch things like an animal and draw in that yellow book he carries."

"Who is this dummy?"

"I don't know. He's deaf and dumb and makes little

squeaks when he's drinking. He's kind of hard to socialize with."

"But he was present when you were talking to Mr. DeAlter and also with the prosecutor and could verify that you did talk with them?"

Skinny thought about it. "I guess."

I looked up at the judge. "I wonder if we could have the sheriff bring this dummy gentleman over when he takes Mr. Stonewaite back. I've no more questions for Mr. Stonewaite now."

Al got to his feet, smiling. "State rests then."

Judge Westley looked down at me. He had a tiny smile and I wondered if he knew what I knew.

"Take Mr. Stonewaite back over and bring back the man Mr. Fort's interested in," Westley said. He leaned back in his chair. "I'm assuming you're calling him in rebuttal?"

"Yes, your honor."

Al got up. "Does this witness understand sign language or something? How can he testify?"

"We'll try to find out," I said soothingly.

At my counsel table Jesse had about given up on me. He watched all drearily.

Carefully, making sure Al didn't see, I gave him the smallest of winks.

The sheriff brought Silent Bill Bottoms back. He came in carrying his yellow pad.

"Would the court swear him in?" I asked.

"How exactly do I do that?" Judge Westley asked.

"Let's put him in front of you. You then tell him to raise his right hand and give him the oath," I suggested.

Westley nodded. I herded Bill in front of him and he

raised his right hand when ordered. Al watched with growing concern. When the oath was finished, Bill nodded his head enthusiastically.

"I'm going to ask him some preliminary questions," I said. "I'm going to tell him to first write down the questions I ask in his yellow pad and then write down his answers."

Al was up. "I'm going to object. It's apparent that Mr. Fort knows more about this witness than I do and the state will need time to find out what's going on."

"Not on a rebuttal witness, your honor."

"Objection overruled. Let's move on."

Al kept standing. I ignored him.

I turned to Silent Bill. "Will you first write out the question I ask and then your answer."

He nodded.

I had him go through name and age and place of residence and when he'd gone into the jail. After each question, when he'd finished his answers, I'd take the yellow pad and hand it up to the court. Each time Al rushed up to the bench and examined question and answer.

Westley finally nodded down at me and at the prosecutor. "Just answers from now on, Mr. Fort. It's apparent this man reads lips and understands your questions."

Al conferred with his deputies while Jesse watched from the counsel table. Jesse was smiling slightly.

"Write only answers now," I instructed.

Silent Bill nodded.

"Did I ask you, while you were in jail, to monitor any conversations between Jesse DeAlter and any other prisoners in the jail?"

Bill wrote one word. "Yes." I showed it to the judge. Al sat in his seat.

Judge Westley said, "Perhaps you should come up here by the bench, Mr. Prosecutor."

Al approached the bench and looked at the yellow pad.

"Did you witness Jesse DeAlter talking to Skinny Stonewaite?"

"Yes."

"Did you witness them talking about the death of Ruth DeAlter?"

This time the scribbled answer took longer. "Skinny asked him about her, but Jesse didn't say anything to him except about Canada."

"Did you constantly watch Mr. DeAlter at all times from when you entered the jail until now?"

"Yes. Except when lights were out and everyone was asleep."

"Did Mr. Stonewaite talk to anyone else other than Mr. DeAlter?"

This time the answer took a while. I read the answer to myself and then handed it to the judge. Al took it and read also.

"That's a lie," he said.

"So that the gentlemen and ladies of the media can better understand what's transpiring, Mr. Bottoms has written answers here which I'll allow them to have. As to the last question Mr. Bottoms replied: "I watched the prosecutor and Skinny. The prosecutor asked if Skinny had heard Mr. DeAlter say anything about his aunt. He then said he'd make it well worth Skinny's while if Skinny could help him out."

The newspeople wrote furiously.

"Your witness," I said to Al.

Al picked up the yellow pad and handed it to Silent Bill.

"You hate me—is that it?"

I had stayed near the bench.

"Might I read the answers he writes?" I asked the court. "It could save time."

"All right," Westley said.

I took the yellow pad. "No."

Al went on, "I've put you in jail before and you want to get even?"

Bill smiled agreeably when he handed me the yellow pad. "I like you. You seem like a nice, fat man."

Someone laughed in the rear of the court. Abe picked that time to enter the courtroom at the rear. He moved silently to our counsel table and took a seat next to Jesse.

"Is Mr. Fort paying you to testify this way?"

A long answer. I read it: "He hired me to go into the jail if I could. I was to watch Mr. DeAlter. I was to watch anyone who tried to talk to him. So that's what I did."

Al's hands were balled tight. I knew what he wanted to do, but I thought I was medium safe inside the courtroom in a crowd.

Al controlled himself. "Did you ever witness Mr. DeAlter saying anything about the death of his aunt?"

Bill hesitated.

"Answer," I encouraged.

Bill wrote for a time. I took the yellow pad and read: "He talked to Mr. Fort about her, but he never said anything about her death. I couldn't read what Mr. Fort said to him, because his back was to me."

"And so was mine?" Al asked.

"No. You got a chair and sat facing me so I could read every word. Thank you."

Al went back to his counsel table. He conferred briefly with his aides.

"That's all," he said finally.

"And I have nothing further," I said. "I would like the court to protect my witness. I'd not want him to have any troubles."

Westley looked out at Goldie, the sheriff. "Can you assure me he'll be all right over in your jail, Sheriff?"

Goldie smiled. "I'll make sure of it, judge. Now that I know he can understand folks, I'll make him a trustee or something. He's a nice boy."

Westley looked at his watch. "I'll listen to the tapes tonight or tomorrow."

"Does that indicate the court might decide this matter before Monday?" Al asked carefully.

"Perhaps," Westley said.

Some of the newspeople had moved up close to the rail to listen.

"I'd like to know, so that I can make whatever announcement I feel is necessary to the press," Al said tartly.

Westley's eyes narrowed. "You can be sure that I'll already have notified the media before I call you, Mr. Windham. That way you can decide, at your leisure, what you want to say."

Al took a step backward. "Now hold on."

Westley smiled. "I'd suggest you do that." He turned to me and ignored the prosecutor. "I hear you had a most harrowing time last night, Mr. Fort. Is it possible that what happened to you might be connected to this case?"

Abe had left the counsel table and now stood beside me.

"I don't know for certain," I said. I twisted the knife in Al. "I'm cautious. I hate to jump to conclusions before I'm certain."

Abe said, "The woman who was in the DeAlter basement and who cut Jack is apparently Peter DeAlter's widow. There was another woman accompanying her. I found her in her hotel room this morning. She got hired out of Chicago to come down here and play a part. She's some kind of retired actress. She says she wasn't hired until after Ruth DeAlter was dead, but that doesn't mean the other woman wasn't in town earlier."

Westley's smile broadened.

My apartment was once the smaller half of an old brick house on Walnut Street, a block off Main. It's good-sized. I have a living room, two bedrooms, a bath with a tub in it almost large enough to be called a swimming pool, and a huge kitchen.

After Abe filled me in on his actions, I went there. Abe told me no more than I'd learned in court.

The house is owned and the other larger part sometimes occupied by a widow lady, Stella Marberry, and her divorced son, Joseph, both aging Scannelsville coal aristocrats, people who split their time between Longboat Key and Scannelsville. I'd observed that a maid came several times a week and cleaned their quarters. Once I'd seen the pair of them in the bank where I do my business and the bank people were doing a lot of bowing and scraping.

Abe told me then, when I asked, that they were very old money.

She favored nineteen-twenties-style dresses with buttons and bows, and she liked her hair done in tight ringlets, dyed red. He wore three-piece suits to the mailbox. They were alert, curious people, very interested in me, their renter.

We'd arrived at a place where we nodded when we met, but rarely spoke. They knew I was a lawyer and that seemingly lent me, in their eyes, a degree of respectability.

Their half of our joint porch was cluttered with things. They had a sturdy swing with an upholstered cushion, two rocking chairs polished to perfection, and a large porcelain-appearing turtle to guard their door. In season, hanging pots swung flowers in all colors at the porch edge when there was a breeze.

They eyed me when I exited my door to meet Abe at the library and then go to Pajama's Place. The weather had gone fine again, cool, but lovely. They were both bundled against it. Almost Florida flight time.

Joseph nodded and I nodded. We smiled. She nodded and smiled last. It was the natural order of such things.

He decided to speak. "Mother and I did not know you were a criminal lawyer when we leased the apartment to you." His tone indicated disapproval.

"I'm usually not. I was appointed by the court," I said.

"I see," he said, not seeing at all, but satisfied. *If the court had done it, then it must be all right.*

"We knew the DeAlters a bit, or rather mother knew Mrs. DeAlter and her brother in the old days. I knew Peter a bit."

I turned to the old lady. She was wearing pink lipstick that had widely missed its mark. She looked old, ugly, and curious all at once.

"Did you know Ruth and Michael well?"

"Not so well. Once, when I was a small girl, I went to a party for Michael." She smiled, remembering. "My mother would never let me associate with him. He had a bad reputation."

I nodded with interest, knowing there was more.

"Michael was the brightest one of them all. He made the money and finished the house. His father started it and then committed suicide in one of the crashes." She gave me a wise look. "Good blood, but violent people. Jesse's the last of the lot. His mother was a romantic and named him after some fine Kentucky poet she once heard speak."

I turned to Joseph. "You said you knew Peter? Do you know Jesse?"

"I knew Peter and saw him once after he left home. I know who Jesse is."

"Where did you see Peter?"

"Someplace. San Francisco perhaps. On the street there."

"Can you remember if it was after the war in Vietnam was over?"

He shook his head, not knowing.

What had seemed promising was fading. "When do you leave for Florida?"

"In ten more days," she said. She shivered in a breeze I found temperate. "It's getting quite cold here."

Joseph nodded. "It's that time. We hope we won't have any truly bad weather before departure." He looked out into the street, bored now. "Someone in the neighborhood has purchased an odd vehicle."

I looked also. Down the street and blocking my old car from view someone had parked a truck with set-down axles and huge tires, its doors so far above the ground that passengers would need to plan how to get inside. The windows were blacked out and the bumpers had to be four or five feet off the ground. I couldn't recognize what make it was. As I watched I also had the feeling once more that I was being watched.

"Not mine," I said.

Joseph nodded approvingly. "I wonder why they do

that sort of thing to them. It seems so useless, but there are scads of them around."

I left my car behind and walked. The day was fading, but the weather just now was January mixed with June.

I could see the river. It was now back down to pool stage. Drift and debris spotted its banks.

I entered the Scannelsville Public Library. I'd made later plans to stop past and pick up Karen, who'd taken an extra day off.

Abe sat in the genealogy room in the rear of the library, his face somber. I entered and he looked up, not really seeing me.

"You liked her," I said, sitting down across from him.

"She fooled me," Abe said. He shook his old head. "I don't like being fooled. But, yes, I was attracted to her. A bright woman. I tried to talk to her this afternoon after the hearing, but she won't see me. The only thing she's told the sheriff is that she came to Scannelsville to see her deceased husband's old home and town and to learn what she could about her chances of getting any of the DeAlter fortune."

"Do you believe that?"

"No. There's more. I want you to look at something with me now."

"What?"

He got up and motioned me to wait. He went to a rack where old school annuals were stored and I watched as he picked some and brought them back to the table.

We were alone.

"Try to find a picture of Peter DeAlter in those," he said. "These are the years he was in high school."

There was a directory in the back which listed names

and the pages where photos with those names could be found. Peter's name appeared seventeen times in the four volumes. I went to each page listed and found that all had been carefully excised from the books.

"No pictures," I said dumbly.

"Right. But excising them out of the books here is silly. There are dozens of people in and around town who still have yearbooks. I ran one down an hour ago and saw a picture of Peter. So why would someone cut them out of these books?"

"I don't know," I said.

"I don't either," he said. "But something or someone seems still to be afoot."

"Let's go to Pajama's and have one drink and talk about it," I said, holding up two fingers.

"Not tonight," he said. "I want to think more on this."

"Did you read all the stuff in my file?" I asked.

"Yes." He grinned. "And Chicken sends you his congratulations on a job well done in court today while I was elsewhere. I came back in just as you were finishing up and didn't comprehend it all, but did do some fancy guessing."

"Thank you. Did you know Teeter Grimes?"

"Vaguely."

"He got run down close to this library," I said.

"And so?"

"It ought to mean something." I thought some more on it, but nothing came.

"It's probably a coincidence," Abe said, looking pensively back down at the table again.

"There have been a lot of coincidences." Something came to me and I pondered it, didn't like it, and let it go. It came back more strongly.

"Do they have a phone in here?" I asked.

"Sure. At the desk and others in the office."

"Can you get Sheriff Goldie to come down here and meet us?"

"Possibly," Abe said.

"I've got a hunch and a new theory."

Twenty minutes later Goldie sat across from us in the genealogy room. Two curious night librarians did their best to stay away from the door.

"You gave me that stuff on Teeter Grimes," I said.

He nodded.

"Tonight Abe was showing me that some books in here had been damaged and all the pictures of Peter DeAlter cut out of them. What if Teeter had seen someone doing that?"

Goldie smiled. "He should have turned whoever it was into the head librarian."

I ignored the sarcasm. "Tell me again how Teeter died, Sheriff."

"A skull fracture, a broken jaw, broken neck. His face was all busted up."

"Did you know him personally, Goldie?"

"Some."

"Was he hard of hearing?"

"Yes. He wore a hearing aid at times."

I remembered the truck parked near my apartment.

"Maybe he never heard what hit him. My guess is he didn't. And what did hit him was either a very big truck or a light truck on raised axles with big, oversized tires."

"It wasn't a huge truck," Goldie said. "That would have left some tire tracks behind. The weather was dry, but there'd been rain. Those big babies carry a lot of weight and the engines are so loud even Teeter would have heard." He shook his head, thinking. "It could have been a 'freaker.'"

"What's a freaker?"

"What you just described, set-down axles, oversized tires."

I thought of something else. "Are there still people keeping check on the DeAlter house?"

"The city boys are checking it every hour or so." He shook his head. "I don't know why or what for, but they're doing it."

"Would you go with Abe and me to the DeAlter basement, either with or without Jesse?"

Goldie gave me a sour look. "You already had me there once today. Early this morning. Why should I go back."

"Because I think Peter's wife or widow, whichever she is, was looking for something and maybe we can find out what it was."

Goldie frowned. "I've heard bull about that place all my young life. The prosecutor made it plain to me after this afternoon's hearing that I wasn't to help you no more. But the bank's the executor and they congratulated me on catching that lady." He looked at Abe. "She still won't say anything and Al has ignored her so far, although one of his deputies did bring me over papers on her today—burglary and assault."

"You want to take a chance?" I asked.

"Maybe."

"Someone was watching the DeAlter house before Ruth died or after she died. Someone breaks in—a someone married to Peter DeAlter, who is either alive or dead. An old fortune is missing. What's it suggest to you?" I asked him.

"Bird dreams," he said and Abe cackled. "But I'll take one more look."

"With Jesse in tow?"

"No. No Jesse. But I'll get me some deputies and meet you there at the house in twenty or thirty minutes."

I called Karen and told her what was to happen. She was intrigued.

"Can you come there and meet me? And also be careful that no one is following you in one of those high-up trucks the sheriff calls 'freakers.' "

"I'll be there," she said.

The basement, lights on, seemed smaller than I remembered it. The wine rack and the heat pumps sat in shadows.

Sheriff Goldie and two deputies stood apprehensively, watching me. I had a small hammer the sheriff had loaned me. I tapped at the walls, but all of them seemed solid. Maybe it was upstairs, but Ruth and the servants had lived up there. And they'd lived there for many years after Michael had died—in the basement.

"Randy here," Goldie said, pointing to one of the deputies. "He was in the construction business and used to carpenter a lot. Maybe he could help you?"

I nodded. It seemed to me that it had to be in the basement. If what was sought was outside, then those looking would be seen. If it was upstairs, then there were people around when it was hidden.

I handed Randy the hammer.

The sheriff glanced around and I was surprised to see him shiver. "I'd just as soon not be here. This place is spooky. I can remember a long time ago that they found Michael dead down here."

I heard what he was saying and imagined that long-ago scene. Michael DeAlter, aging and senile, perhaps with then unrecognized Alzheimer's, dead in the basement. That was when things had fallen apart. There was still money, but no life. Just family hate and cold planning.

Something I'd heard a couple of times came back to me. "Michael was an engineer?"

"That's right," Goldie said.

"An engineer who specialized in mines?"

"Sure. Purdue."

I looked down at the stone floor. It was solid and strong and had been that way for long, long years. I saw no marks in the dust on the floor.

But mining engineers first went downward.

"Randy, try the floor. A mining engineer might think first about tunneling down."

"They went over the floor before," Goldie said. "I know they did because of stories I've heard. It's solid."

"It may be. You got anyone else up in your office or in your reserve deputies you can call in to look?"

"I've got one guy who used to be a foreman at Cratin Number Four."

I looked down at the floor again. "Get him. Get Randy to check and you check and your miner to check. I've got a hunch something's here." I smiled at Goldie. "You might turn out to be a very famous sheriff."

"I'll try. We'll try." He looked down at the stone floor, cunningly fitted together of large stones, and shook his head. But I could see I'd infected him.

"I'm going to my office for a while," I said. "I want to

look over everything one more time. I want to think some. I keep getting ideas and I need to sort them out."

"So we look and you vanish," he said.

"Yes. If you find anything, I'm then going to call Judge Westley and tell him what you found and maybe ask to reopen the bond hearing. I'm also going to call the newspaper, give you the credit, and make it your idea."

"If I do find something or my men find something, then Al is going to be real mad."

"Yes. He will be just that."

We smiled at each other.

"We'll look extra hard," he said when I was at the steps to the outside. "And I got a very large deputy I can have protect me."

I took Karen to my office. I sat her down across the desk. I got out my file and went through it again, making some notes, trying out theories and suspicions. She watched me.

It was now close on nine in the evening.

"They'll call here?" she asked.

"If they find anything worth calling on. Maybe something was there once and now is gone. Maybe there was never anything."

"But who . . ."

"It could be Peter. His wife or widow won't say a thing, so maybe he's hiding out there someplace, waiting us out. The question is why did he send her and not come himself. That makes me believe he isn't out there, that he's dead, and that he told her something before he died, but maybe didn't know all." I thought for a moment. "Maybe one of Jesse's so-called pals, maybe Annie Tinker or Murphy or someone else."

She looked across my desk at me. There was only one

light on, the light on my desk. It captured her eyes. In the dimness the blue seemed black.

I bent back to the file. The old building around me smelled of rot, perhaps part of it coming from the second-hand bookstore on the other side of the thin wall behind me.

We waited. After a while I gave up on the file and closed it. Once, after that, Karen nervously reached out and touched my hand.

"Is Jesse going to get out?"

"Maybe. There's the drug charge also. If the prosecutor loses on this one, you can be sure he'll go after Jesse on the other. But I think I could plead Jesse out and talk the judge into a suspended sentence on the drug bit. Jesse's dried out on alcohol and he hasn't had any drugs for a time and I see no shakes or nerves. He's just Jesse and he needs to discover the rules apply to him also."

"Yes," she said, agreeing.

After a long time the telephone rang. I picked it up and said, "Yes."

Whoever was calling rehung the phone softly. I felt a touch of cold run down my back. It could have been a wrong number.

We sat some more. She was silent and I was silent and content to watch her.

The phone rang again. I picked it up.

"This is Goldie. We got a big mess of stuff down here. One of those floor stones was set in real clever. Randy spotted it because it was darker around the edges from the years than some of the others. It took three of us to lift it up and out, but then Michael was a horse in his day and maybe it was easier then."

"What was in it?" I asked, excited.

"Down below there was a deep hole, maybe seven feet. It was all shelves and there was a lot of stuff. There were some paintings, but they've turned dark and I don't know how much good they'll be."

"Be very careful. Sometimes paintings can be restored."

"It was Michael's safe. All the stuff in it had his name on it. There were old books of stamps and they smell of mold, but look pretty good. Mostly U.S. stuff, but some from other countries. Pretty old. There were lots of coins, mostly gold. There were some big, old books, wrapped carefully."

"You may be sitting on millions of dollars worth of stuff," I said. "Be real careful. Don't move anything that looks fragile."

"Okay. Not knowing for sure you would, I already called the paper. You want to come see it and get your picture taken with mine?"

"No. You take the credit, except I would like you to tell the bank what part I had."

"All right," he said and I thought he sounded relieved. "I took a chance and radioed in and had them set me up to Judge Westley also. He was kind of interested. He said for you to call him yet tonight. And I got half my department and the city boys down here watching."

"Tell them to keep their guns ready. Someone else may be outside wanting very badly what you've found."

"Who?"

"I'm not sure. But someone. Someone may have suspected it was there and killed Ruth DeAlter to empty the house."

"If that's so, we've got her in jail."

"Maybe she isn't all of it. Or maybe she was operating on her own and there's someone else."

"When do you want to see it?"

"Tomorrow is soon enough. In a few minutes I'm going to take Karen over to see Jesse if it's okay with you."

"Fine. Late but fine."

"One more thing," I said. "When the paper gets people there, just remember that all Al gets out of this is egg on his face."

"Count on it."

I hung the phone up. Outside, on Main Street, I could hear the traffic. Karen was smiling.

"How much did they find?"

"A lot. I think Jesse is about to be a wealthy defendant. Let me make one more call."

She nodded.

I called Judge Westley's home number. He answered after a single ring.

"I listened to those grand jury tapes, Jack. All the prosecutor has got is some proximity and leading questions, plus some hearsay. Your man can get out on bond. Let's say fifty thousand."

"He can make that now," I said. "At least he'll be able to come up with it Monday when things get straightened out."

"That's good because it's not official until Monday morning. I'm telling you now so you can plan ahead. The amount I set it at might change, but only downward."

"That's agreeable. Thank you, judge."

"Just how much stuff is in that hole in the basement the sheriff is so excited about?"

"I'm not sure. It went in there when rarities were a lot cheaper than now. I'll know more later."

He laughed. "Well, maybe the county can get out of this one feewise and Jesse can pay you."

"I'd think so," I said. "And thanks again."

I hung up the phone and leaned back in my seat. "Bond will be set somewhere in the neighborhood of fifty thousand dollars on Monday morning."

Karen smiled, very excited.

Outside the traffic noise grew suddenly intense. I heard the thumping of tires and the whine of a motor. Too near. It came to me too late what the sound might be. I jumped to my feet.

There were sounds of splintering and breaking from the front office where Fran's desk was. I saw the ceiling above me bow and crack.

I caught at Karen and pulled her to me. The office was reception room first, then my office, then Abe's. We could go out in the hall and maybe retreat into Abe's.

My wall bowed in and split aside and I saw the huge truck, lights on bright, as it waded through and over the debris.

The driver tried to cut it toward us, but it was too much of a turn.

I remembered something. The used-book store was behind us. I found a place between the studs and hit it very hard, tearing into the thin plasterboard. I kicked at the hole that was opened. The hole widened. Behind me I could hear the driver, backing and turning. He hunted for us with his lights.

I pushed Karen through the hole and followed behind. The truck driver blared his horn at us.

Karen and I were in the midst of stacks of old magazines and shelves of books. We moved between them. The lights behind us dimmed and then brightened.

The truck came through the wall.

In the light I could see the shelves buckle and fall, raining down on the truck. I could see Defoe and Twain and Westlake falling and bouncing, clogging the floor and making it difficult for the truck to rear over them.

I found the front door of the secondhand bookstore. I tried it and it was jammed from the damage that had been done to the front of the building. I got a firm hold on the handle and twisted and pulled the protesting door open.

We fled around the corner of the building.

"Run to the sheriff's office," I called to Karen. I tried to keep pace with her, but like most, she was faster. We crossed the side street and found trees and tried to hide behind them as we ran.

It was too open. He'd catch us here.

I heard motor sounds move from the building we'd fled. The sounds came back out into the open and to the street. Once the sound died, but then caught again. If he turned our way, he'd have us. For a time I thought the driver followed, but then the sounds receded and died.

We ran on toward the jail.

Once inside I told the story to a deputy while Karen shivered beside me. I waited while he went to his radio and put the word out.

When that was done, I waited some more.

Goldie finally came on the radio. "You in trouble again, Fort?"

"Someone tried to run us down with one of those freakers," I said. "Tore up Abe's office and the used bookstore next doors."

"I'll be up to take a look. But it'll be a while."

"That's okay. We're safe here."

"I'm not sure you're safe anywhere," he said.

The deputy went back to the television screens that showed the cells.

"You go back and tell Jesse what's going on," I said. "Tell him I think we'll get him out next week early and that I think I might be able to get him a suspended on the drug deal. Tell him the sheriff's found Michael's money—lots of it. That should make his day."

She nodded, the excitement of the escape and the found money in her eyes. "All right. But you go with me."

"No. I need to call Abe and tell him what's happened, especially about his building."

"Yes," she said and I found it impossible to read her eyes. "I'll tell Jesse."

I called Abe and we talked. After that I waited in the jail office for a while longer. Karen didn't come. The deputy let me look into the television screen that showed Jesse's cell. She was standing close to the cell door, holding his hand. Across the way Silent Bill watched them, smiling.

After another while I got a deputy to take me home and watch me go inside.

I slept lightly. If anyone other than Mildred Marsh wanted what had been in the basement of the DeAlter mansion under the stones, they now must know it wasn't going to happen that way. I thought maybe someone might come calling for me.

But no one came. The phone rang a few times. Once it was an excited local newsman asking me questions. Another time it was someone from the bank saying that he'd been to the jail after viewing the basement hoard and that Jesse had told him he wanted me to be the attorney to handle his father's estate. I promised gratefully that I'd come in and get things going on Monday.

Karen didn't call. Not that weekend.

On Monday morning at nine, after talking earlier with the bank people, I was in Judge Westley's court.

I waited for a while for the prosecutor to appear. There were some newspeople hanging around in the corridor. I talked vaguely with them.

They brought Jesse over at nine-thirty and we waited in the courtroom. Al didn't come. Eventually one of his deputies arrived.

Sheriff Goldie had Jesse in single custody. The chains and manacles were gone. Jesse smiled at me.

"You did well," he said charmingly, "very well."

I sat him down beside me and waited for Judge Westley to enter.

Westley took the bench and nodded out at us. The courtroom was half full, the largest crowd I'd yet seen there.

"Where's Mr. Windham?" the judge asked the deputy prosecutor, the one called Curly.

"He sent me over to cover," the deputy said. He looked down at the counsel table.

Westley smiled. "I find, after reviewing the evidence against the defendant, that it's not strong or convincing and I'm going to set bond on the defendant at ten thousand dollars."

Ten thousand dollars was almost too low, an insult and a dare to the prosecutor. The deputy got to his feet, gulped twice, and sat back down.

I saw some reporters smiling. The word had passed about what Al had tried to do in court with Skinny and what I'd done to offset it.

I got up. "Your honor, the bank has been in touch with me this morning and Mr. DeAlter is about to inherit a substantial sum of money which will allow him not only to make his bond, but also to pay his legal fees."

"How much is substantial?" Westley asked.

"Perhaps as much as a thousand times the amount of his bond, perhaps more. He'd be foolish to flee. Would the court allow him to sign his own bond?"

"Who will sign as surety?"

"I asked the bank and they've agreed so to do."

Goldie smiled up at Judge Westley. "I'll accept it that way if you've no objections, your honor."

Westley gave Goldie and the rest of us a stern look and then a smile. He tapped his gavel lightly. "All right. So be it."

I walked back to the office. Abe had made weekend arrangements and someone was already at work covering the huge hole in the office front. Carpenters and other workmen worked here and there. I got through them and walked down to Abe's office, still whole, but lopsided. I could hear Abe on the phone making Florida arrangements with a travel agent. Clearwater, the sun, and bridge, bridge, bridge!

He saw me at the door. He winked, finished his conversation, and hung up.

"I gave the secretary a couple of days off. They'll have us back in biz here inside of a week. We got lots of insurance."

"Good. Then you're off to Florida?"

"Yep. But first here's a telegram from my friendly congressman on Peter DeAlter. Came a bit ago, too late for the fireworks." He handed it to me.

I read the telegram and read it again. "Peter DeAlter, killed in action near Da Nang, January 2, 1971."

"How about his widow?"

"She's still sitting silently in jail," Abe said. "She's never said another word." He thought for a moment. "Goldie printed her and sent this off over the weekend. Maybe she's wanted someplace else." He shook his head. "I'm kind of sorry for her."

I felt my forehead. I'd taken the tape off yesterday and all there was was a fine, brown line up near my hair.

"Did she kill Ruth?" Abe asked.

"Maybe."

I had no office and no secretary and so I went out and wandered aimlessly. Some people nodded and some didn't. Nothing much had changed.

I went back to the courthouse. The rush was done for the day in court and no one was around but Chicken. He sat smiling at me in his office.

"You ought to be happy," he said. "I know the judge is. The town is telling and retelling the story out there and Al Windham is as dead politically as Ruth DeAlter is literally. I, we, owe you one."

"One of what?" I asked.

"One whatever. Ain't nobody ever been able to put the prosecutor out and down before. You did it once and now you've done it again, this time real hard. You beat him at his own jail game."

"I think someone's still out there, Chicken. I feel it."

He shook his head. "They found a burned-out freaker truck early this morning on one of the county roads. It got stole Thursday. Some are saying it might have been Peter DeAlter who had it and that now he's run. They think the woman in jail will crack and tell."

"Could be. You say you owe me one. Want to repay it?"
He nodded gravely.

I asked Al to meet me at the courthouse. I called his office and told him I had information about Peter DeAlter and that I'd share it with him. I had the telegram, of course.

We made arrangements to meet in the open courtroom at four. By the time I got there, Westley was leaving his office. Chicken's room was dark.

Westley nodded to us in the hall. "You boys lock things when you're finished," he ordered. "Do you need me for anything?"

"No," I said. "Thank you, your honor."

Al frowned hard at Westley's retreating back. He then looked me over. "You said you had some information for me?"

"Yes." I handed him the telegram. He read it and handed it back.

"What's it mean? All you're showing me are government records that may or may not mean something." He shook his head. "I heard about your troubles up at Abe's office. Someone's after you, Fort."

"I guess so."

"And all this stuff they found isn't going to keep me from going after Jesse on the drug charge."

"You may have some trouble on that," I said. "In the first place Jesse accepted no pay when it was offered. In the second place whoever winds up representing him might very well plead him out and ruin the fun." I thought for a moment. "Or force you to trial. Jesse can buy all the big-time legal help, expert witnesses and the like he needs with his multi-bucks."

He watched me, his eyes careful. "I go off half-cocked sometimes. I should have checked better on you after you bloodied me in court that first time. I didn't. Now I have. I called the firm you worked for in Chicago. They told me you were their number-one trial man and they'd take you back in a minute. Why'd you leave there and come here to bother me in this backwater town?"

"Got tired of the big city," I said.

"I also found out you got shot out of the sky in Vietnam and that's why you walk funny."

I nodded.

"I've got the woman in jail and sooner or later one of two things will happen. She'll start talking or someone will try to get her out. My guess is she came to town and stuck the pillow over Ruth's face so that she could get into the house and steal what was there."

I nodded and waited.

"Or maybe it was the servants and the woman we've got in jail found out Ruth was dead and then came here. Or maybe it was someone else who did Ruth in and we'll never know who it was."

"I think if Peter was alive and well, then he'd have been in that basement with her. The only way I see him being alive now is if something disabling happened to him in Vietnam and he couldn't be with her. And the telegram doesn't give us any indication of that," I said.

Al watched me. Outside the courtroom windows a fine, thin rain had begun to fall. The wind blew it against the window. Only one bank of lights was on and the courtroom was silent and empty.

"I may take another look at the servants and the people Jesse hung with."

"Yes. You could do that. You didn't do it before, but I

imagine you will now, one way or another." I looked at him and watched his face. "Want to hear my theory?"

"Not particularly, but I'll listen."

"I think you killed her, Al. You drew her will and maybe something happened when she signed it or afterward that gave you the idea she was about to switch lawyers again. You needed her money. Maybe you know the woman in jail, maybe not. Maybe you and the woman had something going on what was in the house, but I doubt it now. If she wanted to get in the house, you, as attorney for the executor, could have gotten her in."

"I never met her," he said, "so dream on."

"You needed the money from the estate which you'd be paid for settling it. So you went to her room, found out you were about to be replaced, and killed her. You thought you had Jesse in a box, but you made some alternate plans if you didn't. You knew Jesse was in the house. You could put him in jail for dealing cocaine and get him indicted by a tame grand jury for murder. You'd kill a lot of birds with a single stone. You'd get money to campaign with, you'd get yourself a sensational case, and you'd continue the upward political path."

"Say a word of this in public and I'll sue you."

I shrugged. "I'll say it and let you sue. I bet I can put you at her place the night she died. You watched your state trooper make a buy. You dismissed the drug case against Jesse when you got your indictment. You didn't want the state cop telling you were at or near Ruth's house. Judge Westley got a note. I'll bet you did also. No mention of it was made in the grand jury tapes. Then Ruth's will was by her bed. Who else would she talk to about it but you? Not Jesse because he got only a minor bequest. Not the servants. So you. You'd undoubtedly been in the house be-

fore because she seldom went outside it. So you climbed
her stairs unseen, opened her door, and when you found
your fears were real, you put a pillow over her head. You
were lucky, or at least you thought you were. You got in
and out and then you went hard after Jesse."

"Pile of crap," he said.

"Maybe, but I think you planned it. There was a chance
Jesse might wake up and that worried you. You'd then
have to kill him also. So you went to the library and set
yourself up a smoke screen by removing all of the pictures
of Peter DeAlter from the yearbooks. I think Teeter
Grimes saw you there, maybe even saw you slicing pages
out of the yearbooks. You talked him into silence, but you
knew he was nosy and unreliable. So he had to die. Someplace out in the county you borrowed or stole a freaker
truck, mashed him with it, and either hid the truck or
cleaned it up and returned it. You're a man who goes back
to things that have been successful for him in the past. You
did it with the prisoner you tried to use against Jesse.
When I started sniffing close, you got either the same
truck or another one and came after me."

"You should be committed," he said. He was smiling a
thin little smile.

"You'll fall, Al. You're well known. Once the story starts
to circulate, then someone in this small town and county
will have seen you under puzzling circumstances, or one
of the servants will remember that Ruth was about to
change lawyers. And of course someone already has seen
you." I reached in my pocket and got him one of the
copies of the note I'd been given by Judge Westley.

He read it, crumpled it, and put it in his pocket.

"There are other copies including the one you got," I
said.

"I'm prosecutor here," he said. "I run this town."

"You're only a piece of old meat drying in the winter cold. You won't be able to get elected to anything once I begin talking. Whether you get convicted or not, you're dead in this area."

I saw his eyes. He'd moved up closer to me as we'd talked.

"What I'll do now is pitch you out a window. I'll mash you up enough first so that you'll not feel a thing when you hit. I'll tell them you jumped. No one will question me. No one will dare. I'm the law here. This county operates on Windham's law."

"You killed Ruth then?"

"Too late for you to have a need to know, Fort."

"But I'm curious. I'm right, aren't I?"

"Sure. Except for the woman in the basement. I never knew her. I did what I needed to do to make the world work for me. And I'd have got Jesse and would be off free if you'd not nosed around and put that deaf and dumb bastard in jail and set him to watch." He eyed me with relish. "You're too damned slow to run from me, Fort. Maybe I'll put a pen mark on you for fun before I drop you. It was a good idea last time."

I stepped back behind a counsel table, the one closest to the window, but he followed. One huge hand reached for me to draw me close. I hit him very hard and he grunted, but kept coming. There was muscle under that fat.

He laughed triumphantly. "I work out too, small man," he said.

A voice behind him said, "So do I."

Al jumped and turned. Chicken smiled at him. He was holding a large revolver.

"I used to lift and shot-put guys like you," Chicken said. "Now I'm older, so I blow holes in them."

Al stepped away. I could see him figuring out his response. His hands went down to his sides.

"Both of you hate me. If the Cannell County world outside doesn't know it now, they will when I get done." He shook his head. "Where were you hiding when this was going on?"

"Under the judge's bench, dear prosecutor. Cramped, but close. And I heard every word."

"You tell your side and I'll tell mine," Al said. "I'm leaving now. Both of you had better think long and hard before you try or say anything."

Chicken nodded. "Leave then," he said cheerfully.

Al moved quickly. I heard him down the hall and to the stairs. Soon all sound stopped.

"I did one thing you didn't tell me to do," Chicken said. He led me to the court reporter's desk in front of the bench. A recording device winked its lights to me. Chicken reached down and turned it off and popped out a cassette into his big hands. He flipped it, right hand to left, then back again.

"He was wrong. There's you, me, and a recording," he said. "In a while we'll assemble a crowd and play it for them. Sheriff, judge, chief of police. I don't know what you do legally when a prosecutor goes bad, but I'll bet there's a remedy." He flipped the cassette up and caught it one more time. "And this town now doesn't operate on Windham's law. It operates on Fort's law."

He put the cassette in an inside pocket. He whopped me on the back, immensely satisfied.

I found I wasn't too proud to take on Michael DeAlter's long-delayed estate. Some of the paintings and all of the old rare books were salvageable, most of the stamps were good ones, and some of the coins were very rare. The bank estimated twelve million.

Peter DeAlter's widow hired an out-of-town lawyer and filed an action to set Michael's will aside, but from what I read, she seemed to have little chance. Someone, not Peter, did make a bond for her after a time.

I saw Jesse once more. He came to my office the day Al Windham was arrested for murder after being indicted by a grand jury called by a special prosecutor.

"I'm going to take a trip," he said. "Do you think the bank would give me an advance?"

I called and listened and it was easy. "They'll make you a loan for whatever you want. They can't make a partial distribution until Peter's wife's claim is finished."

"Pay her something if you want," he said. "It's okay with me."

"Okay."

"I'm going to take a trip, but I'll stay in touch. I want to take another look at me and the world."

"Sure."

"You did me well, Jack. I appreciate it."

I wondered about Karen, but I wasn't going to question him.

"Good luck," I said simply.

"You made my luck for me. Maybe now I can make some more for myself. With Al out of office I've been informed they may not go after me on the drug charge."

"I didn't know that."

He looked down at the floor. "I got into drugs because it was something to do, another way for me to screw up things." He laughed at himself and I liked him better for laughing. "Now I'm a man of substance instead of substance abuse."

I waited.

He shook my hand again, said he'd be in touch, and went out the door.

Abe went on to Florida. I went to the office and to my apartment. I also went to Pajama's a few times. Doc Jacobsen viewed me with restored good humor and invited me to go with him in the spring to Churchill Downs. I smiled and told him I'd let him know.

Ten days later after the night Michael's fortune was found, my doorbell rang at night. I went to the door and turned on my outer light.

Karen DeAlter stood outside in the cold.

My neighbors had left that morning for Longboat Key, but I opened the door quickly and turned off the outer light. There were other neighbors.

"Hello," she said gravely.

"Hi."

"May I come in?"

"Of course you can." I let her enter, stepping aside.

She stood in front of me. "I made Jesse a promise when I went to the jail that last night. I told him I'd do nothing about either him or you for ten days. That time will be up in about two minutes, but I like to keep my promises."

"Can I take your coat?" I asked.

She looked carefully at her watch. "Not quite yet. He invited me to go on a trip with him—a long trip. I thought on that and all the money he'll be getting. I wanted, in some ways, to go. I've had the thin of it with him and I thought maybe I should have some of the thick."

"A lot of money," I said. "Very old dollars."

"Yes, I know." She looked down at her watch. "But I've decided to stay." She held out her arms invitingly and her blue eyes gleamed. "We could get things started by taking off this coat. You never know what you'll find under it."

So I took off her coat.

About the Author

Joe L. Hensley has written for many magazines, in both the science fiction and mystery fields. He is the author of ten previous novels for the Crime Club, including *Robak's Firm, Robak's Fire,* and *Robak's Cross.* Judge Hensley lives in Madison, Indiana.

FORT'S LAW
JOE L. HENSLEY

A juicy family murder with big money at stake is always the kind of crime that scandalizes a small town, and the type of case that can make or break a country lawyer's reputation. That's the challenge Jack Fort takes on when he is appointed to defend Jesse DeAlter, a handsome and privileged young man accused of murdering his very old, very rich aunt.

Brash and arrogant, Jesse is a hard man to defend. Everyone in town knows that his relations with his aunt were less than congenial, and his penchant for drug and alcohol abuse makes him seem perfectly capable of violence. To make matters worse, Fort is in love with the woman Jesse married—and he's not quite sure he wants to see his client set free.

However, Fort is determined to defeat Al Windham, a politically